the Wedding Rescue

IVY LAYNE

GINGER QUILL PRESS, LLC

The Wedding Rescue

Written by Ivy Layne as Alexa Wilder, originally published as Alexa Wilder

Copyright © 2015 by Alexa Wilder

All rights reserved.

No part of this book may be reproduced in any form or by any electronic or mechanical means including information storage and retrieval systems, without permission in writing from the author. The only exception is by a reviewer, who may quote short excerpts in a review.

This book is a work of fiction. Names, characters, places, and incidents either are products of the author's imagination or are used fictitiously. Any resemblance to actual persons, living or dead, events, or locales is entirely coincidental.

Find out more about the author and upcoming books online at
www.ivylayne.com

CONTENTS

ALSO BY IVY LAYNE

Scandals of the Bad Boy Billionaires

The Billionaire's Secret Heart (Novella)

The Billionaire's Secret Love (Novella)

The Billionaire's Pet

The Billionaire's Promise

The Rebel Billionaire

The Billionaire's Secret Kiss (Novella)

The Billionaire's Angel

Other Books By Ivy Layne

The Wedding Rescue

The Courtship Maneuver

The Temptation Trap

Don't Miss Out on New Releases, Exclusive Giveaways, and More!!

Join Ivy's Readers Group!

ivylayne.com/readers-group

CHAPTER ONE

DYLAN

I saw her across a crowded room. It's such a cliché, especially for me. I see beautiful women across crowded rooms all the time. The Delecta was my casino, and she was sitting at my bar.

It's hard to say what made me stop. She wasn't a showgirl or a model, and nothing like the tall, skinny, overly made up women I was accustomed to. No, she was something else. She was *real*.

When was the last time I'd had real? Real curves, generous enough to have her hips straining the seams of her navy blue dress. I wanted to sink my fingers into those hips while I fucked her from behind.

Real tits. Had to be. They were soft and full, even from a distance. They, too, strained against her dress. Mouthwatering. And her lips. Plump. Perfectly shaped to wrap around my cock. I had to see more.

I eased into the bar, busy enough for six o'clock on a Thursday, but not as crowded as it would be in a few hours. I needed a better angle to see her face.

From the door, all I got was long, shining, dark hair, streaming down her back in loose waves, a hint of her lips, the curve of an eyebrow, and nothing else. Did her face live up to the promise of her body? I was going to find out.

I crossed the room to the bar, nodding at a few people as I went. Sliding into the seat beside her, I raised a finger for the bartender.

"Sir," he said with a deferential nod. I waved it away. This wasn't the time to impress her with my status. Not until I knew if she'd be impressed.

She might be one of those anti-corporate types, in which case being a billionaire wasn't going to help me get her in my bed. And the closer I got, the more certain I was. However her night had begun, it would end with me.

I ordered a Manhattan. At the sound of my voice, she turned to look at me. Fucking perfect. Her face was as real as her body. No dramatic cheekbones or startling blue eyes caked with mascara. No, she barely wore any make-up. Not even lipstick.

Her grey eyes were clear and intelligent, and her sweet, rosy lips had a natural pout. Her dark brows matched her hair. When her eyes met mine, they widened. For a second, she looked like a deer caught in headlights. Or one who'd spotted a predator far too close and knew he'd locked on.

Her instincts told her all she needed to know. She was in danger and there was no escape.

Then I saw it. The red rims of her eyes, the streak of moisture on her cheek. A primal part of me felt a bolt of satisfaction.

She'd been crying. The tears were a weakness, and my way in. With all the resources at my disposal, whatever problem she had, I would fix it. Then she'd be mine for however long I wanted her.

CHAPTER TWO

LEIGHA

I was well into my second appletini when I heard the chair next to me slide back. I kept my eyes on the bar, not interested in company or polite chitchat. My calm, orderly, sedate life was in a shambles, and I had no interest in talking to anyone except the bartender.

That is, until I heard his voice. It was low and dark, like hot chocolate with caramel drizzled on top, and it sent shivers down my spine. He had to be hot. No one with a voice like that could be anything else.

I snuck a peek and froze. Holy crap. Hot didn't begin to cover it. Our eyes met and I couldn't move, couldn't turn away.

His eyes were the crisp, fresh green of a Granny Smith apple. I'd never seen eyes like that before. On anyone else I might have wondered if they were contacts, but not on this man. His eyes were extraordinary, but serious.

This man didn't put up with bullshit. Not one who'd wear colored lenses. His face could have come out of a magazine, with his thick, dark hair, those bladed cheek-bones, and that full lower lip.

But he lacked the empty blandness of a model in an advertisement. No, his face had character. He had fine lines around his mouth that suggested he laughed a lot. A tan that said he liked to be outdoors. His gaze was assessing, evaluating me. I wanted to tear my eyes away and look anywhere else, but I couldn't.

He wasn't just a regular guy. I knew that already. Spinal shivers from his voice aside, the bartender had called him 'Sir' when he'd come in.

And that suit. I didn't know a ton about fashion, but it was too well tailored not to be custom made. He was way out of my league—way, way out.

"Bad day?" he asked in that chocolate and caramel voice. More shivers ran down my spine. A suspicious heat grew between my legs. Women would pay just to hear this guy talk.

"Bad week," I said, my mouth moving before I could stop it.

"Do you want to talk about it?"

The bartender delivered his drink, and he took a sip, eyes still on mine. He waited with all the patience in the world to hear my pathetic story.

Suddenly, I was less depressed and more ashamed. How had I let my life come to this?

"I'm sure you have better things to do than listen to a stranger's problems," I said, not wanting this beautiful man to know what a mess I was.

"I'm never too busy to listen to an attractive woman," he answered. I snorted a laugh, choking a little on my apple-tini. He must be working an angle. Men like this didn't hit on me.

Maybe he thought I was, easy, or maybe he was another scammer. I'd had enough of that lately. I couldn't afford to be taken in again.

"Smooth," I said, still giggling a little. "But whatever you're selling, I don't need any. I've got enough trouble as it is."

"I'm not selling anything." He actually looked affronted, as if I'd insulted him. "Really. I just got off work, wandered in here, saw you, and wanted to get to know you better."

"Why?" I challenged, tossing back the rest of my drink.

Sure, this was the most beautiful man I'd seen in real life. However, his sitting beside me and starting a conversation just because he liked the way I looked was a little hard to swallow.

Girls like me did not attract men like him. I was too plump, too boring, and too plain. Besides, I was not having a lucky week. Or month, if we're being honest.

"Because," he said, leaning in so his lips almost grazed my ear, "you're the only real thing I've seen in this place in months. You're gorgeous, and you don't even know it. And I want to know you better."

I snorted again. Not the most elegant sound. Maybe I'd had one drink too many—no, I'd definitely had one too many. I just couldn't buy it. I had decent self-esteem, but come on.

This guy could get any woman he wanted. I was a somewhat overweight accountant who lived in a tiny bungalow, drove a beige sedan, and contributed regularly to her retirement account.

All I was missing was a few cats, and I'd be all ready to become a little old lady at twenty-five. I might live in Vegas, but it could have been the small midwestern town I'd grown up in for the all the excitement in my life.

"Sorry. Not interested," I said. "The last hot guy who told me I was gorgeous ended up cleaning out my savings account. That was after telling me how hard it was to date such a fat ass long enough to get my bankcard and pin. I'm not looking for a guy like you."

I waved my hand in the air in a gesture meant to encompass all that was him. "I need a nice, boring guy. Maybe another accountant. Or an actuary. Someone like that."

"How much did he get?"

I sat back, startled. All the smooth had drained from his face. It was like looking at a different man. His arresting green eyes were narrowed, his lips tight. He looked pissed and even though I knew it wasn't directed at me, he was a little scary.

Why had I told him that? My most humiliating secret and I blurted it out to a complete stranger? I had second thoughts about ordering another drink.

"Ten thousand," I mumbled, flushing with embarrassment. I'd been stupid, and I'd paid for it.

"How did he get it?" His voice was hard. Uncompromising. I thought about not answering, but I didn't have it in me to stay silent, especially not with that commanding tone in his luscious voice.

"It was a back-up savings account. Not the one attached to my checking. But it had a bank card. I never used the card, and all the info was in a file in my office. He found it and stole the card. Then he made the maximum withdrawal every day until it was empty. I only check the account once a month, so I missed it. I feel so stupid."

To my horror, I felt another tear escape from the corner of my eye. He reached up and brushed it away with one warm, gentle fingertip.

"Don't cry," he said. "Did you go to the police?"

"They weren't that interested. He said it was a gift, he had the card and the PIN, and we'd just broken up when I reported it. So they filed it as a domestic issue and suggested I sue him."

"Did you?"

My shoulders slumped. "I started to. Then my lawyer found out that 'Steven' wasn't actually Steven. And he'd disappeared. So there was no one to sue. And I was out the lawyer's fees, which I couldn't exactly afford with no savings to fall back on. I have a good job, but not good enough to replace ten grand overnight."

I changed my mind about the drink and raised my hand to get the attention of the bartender. If I was going to get through this night, I needed another drink, stat.

Something stronger than an appletini. Tequila? To my surprise, the god of a man sitting beside me took my hand in his and pulled it down before the bartender could notice.

"You don't need another drink," he said. "You need something to eat. I'm taking you to dinner." He slid off his chair, apparently assuming I'd follow right behind.

"I do need another drink." I tried to raise my hand again, but he hadn't let it go. "And I can't go to dinner with you. I'm eating dinner in an hour."

"Date?" he asked, eyes narrowed. This time, I really couldn't help my snort of disgusted laughter.

"Are you kidding? It's going to be a long time before I'm dating again. No. My sister is getting married here this weekend and I have to meet her, my other sister and my mother for dinner." I scowled at the thought of the other reason I was having a miserable week.

"Fine. Then I'll take you for appetizers."

Before I knew it, he'd tucked my arm in his and was leading me out of the bar. What was going on? Was I just going to let him drag me out of the bar? When I didn't jerk my arm away or tell him off, I realized I was.

Why not? I'd missed lunch and I could use a snack before dinner. God forbid I actually ate anything in front of my sisters. I'd never hear the end of it. Even so, I put up a token resistance.

"I can't go to eat with you."

"Why not?" he asked, easily.

"I don't even know your name," I protested. He stopped walking and turned to face me.

"Dylan Kane." He held out his hand to shake, watching me carefully, as if waiting for something. When I didn't respond, except to take his hand, he smiled.

I almost missed the smile, jolting a little at the touch of his skin to mine. His hand was warm and strong, the touch sending tingles all over, settling in my breasts and between my legs.

That was a lot of impact for a simple handshake. A few more of those, and my panties would be soaked. This guy was dangerous. I wondered what it would feel like if he touched me.

No. I was not going there. Thinking with my hormones was how I got into trouble with Steven. I was not going to make any more lust driven decisions.

Instead of drifting off into fantasies of those warm, strong hands all over my body, I squeezed his hand back and said, "Leigha Carmichael."

"Leigha," He repeated. "A beautiful name." Pulling me close to his side again, he led us further into the casino. We headed for the bank of elevators, away from the restaurants.

I tried to reclaim my arm. I'd said I'd go eat with him, but it didn't seem like a great idea to disappear into the upper floors with a man I just met. Cautious, that was me.

Except I'd been cautious with Steven, and here I was, broke and alone. Before I could protest, he asked,

"Is there anything you don't eat?"

I shook my head and said, "No." He lifted his mobile to his ear and hit a button before he spoke.

"Cheryl, order in a selection of appetizers. I'll be there in a minute with company."

Now I did try to pull my arm away. "I'm not going to your room with you." He grinned at me, relaxed and amused.

"No, you're not. At least not right now. We're going to my office. It's private, comfortable, but you won't be completely alone with me."

"Your office? You work here?" I asked, glancing around the floor of the casino.

The Delecta was one of the newest casinos on the strip. Sumptuous and elegant, it was not a family casino. It was on the small side, with more suites than the average hotel, all of them luxurious and expensive.

So expensive, I'd told my sister I'd rather stay at home and drive in for the wedding events. But, as usual, she pitched a fit, the rest of the family took her side, and I found myself convinced to spend money I didn't have on a pricey hotel room in my own city. I'd managed to get one of the single rooms and stuck it on my emergency credit card.

The Delecta was a casino for adults. The spa was extensive, the decor designed to seduce, and everywhere I looked I saw couples, exquisitely dressed and beautifully groomed, gambling away their money and laughing with delight as they did it.

This place was the ultimate scam. Didn't they know the house always won? And here I was, wandering off with a man I didn't know, just because he was beautiful and charming. So who was I to judge?

I looked up to see that he was smiling at me, an almost fond expression on his face.

"You really don't know who I am, do you?" he asked. Should I? I could tell now that I should. I didn't get out a ton. Was I making a fool of myself? Probably.

"No, I don't," I admitted. "Sorry." I shrugged apologetically.

"I own the Delecta," he said. "Well, I'm part owner of the conglomerate that owns the Delecta. But, for the last few years, this project has been my baby. I do most of my work from here."

"You own the Delecta?" I felt my jaw hanging open. So not just panty melting hot, but a billionaire? As in, actually having and controlling assets worth multiple billions of dollars?

I was so completely out of my league. I was a junior accountant in a modestly-sized firm. This man could have his arms draped in supermodels in the blink of an eye.

"I own Kane Enterprises, which owns the Delecta, yes." He steered me into an empty elevator while I stared and tried to absorb this information. What was he doing with me?

CHAPTER THREE

DYLAN

She didn't get it, and why would she? That just made my task easier. I understood women, got their strange thoughts about men and food and their appearance.

I knew way too much about the affect money and power had on some of them. I knew the grasping and the lies, their need to take. I'd see soon enough if this girl was one of those.

I doubted it. She probably thought she was overweight and boring, wondering why I'm not calling up a showgirl or a model instead of her. By the time I was finished with her, she'd know the truth.

She was luminous, her creamy skin soft under my hand, her grey eyes clear and honest. Her tits jiggled a little with every step, her rounded hips moved with a natural, sensual sway.

Just the idea of getting her naked, seeing all that sweet flesh bare, was enough to get my cock half-hard. She had to be in her mid-twenties, but she radiated innocence. I missed innocence.

Lately, I'd come to crave it, to need the clean feel of someone who wasn't scheming. I missed people who weren't trying to get something from me.

I looked her over as she shifted from one foot to the other, too shy to meet my eyes. Delicious. I couldn't decide where to start—with those soft, full, perfect tits?

Would she be one of those women who could come just from having her tits sucked? From the way she shivered when I touched her, I bet she would.

Or I could shock her, and go straight for that sweet pussy. I guessed it saw little use. If she'd seen a lot of action, she would have been more at ease with her body. This girl was barely a woman, and she had no idea what she was, and what she could be.

I was the man who was going to show her.

CHAPTER FOUR

LEIGHA

I kept my mouth shut all the way to his office, not sure what to say. I felt less anxious about being alone with him, at least in the sense of safety. The head of Kane Enterprises wouldn't bring me to his office if he planned to hurt me.

I still didn't understand what he was doing with me. I wished I would have had another drink, but I was wobbling a little in my heels, and knew he was right. What I needed was food.

The elevator doors opened to an elegant reception area, done in sleek grey with black and red accents, the same colors as the hotel. Behind the desk sat a gorgeous blonde in a trim black suit, her pale hair in a neat twist.

This was the kind of woman I'd expect to see with Dylan. She was polished, beautiful, composed, and devastatingly sexy. At the sound of the door opening, she came to her feet.

"Mr. Kane," she said. "Your food will be delivered shortly."

"Thank you, Cheryl. Please hold any calls."

I barely caught her nod before he ushered me through the tall, black double doors that led to his office. The single room was bigger than my entire bungalow. His desk was enormous, lacquered black wood with a matching leather desk chair behind it.

A flat screen television was mounted on the wall opposite the desk, viewable from the black leather sofa and matching chairs that faced the window facing the door.

The plate-glass window made up the entire wall, offering a panoramic view of Vegas and the desert beyond. I stopped and stared for a moment, taking in the luxury around me.

"I'd offer you wine," he said, drawing my attention, "but I think a coffee might be more in order." He raised an eyebrow, inviting my opinion.

"Please," I said. Coffee was a great idea. Some caffeine would clear the hot guy haze, and wash away some of the alcohol.

Okay, it wouldn't do anything about the alcohol, but at least it would make me more alert. I had the feeling I'd need to be alert with Dylan Kane. He pressed a button on his desk phone.

"Cheryl, two cappuccinos, please." Turning to the couch, he gestured to the comfortable seats. "Please, sit."

Again, I did as he ordered. What was it about him? I could be a pleaser. I knew that about myself. But normally I wouldn't be jumping at the commands of a stranger.

I'd maybe obey my boss without thinking. But a man I'd just met? There was something about the way Dylan spoke that captivated me, making me do as he said.

He was a charming man, obviously raised to be incredibly polite. But, though he said 'please', it was clear he wasn't asking. And something about that was intriguing.

Ever since he'd touched my face in the bar, my body had been humming at his presence. I wanted him to touch me again. I knew it wasn't wise, but I wasn't sure I cared.

Dylan sat beside me, stretching his legs out in front of him. He leaned back into the couch, one arm across the back, fingertips almost grazing my shoulder.

My shy side, usually in charge, told me to lean forward, out of range. I didn't listen. I wanted to feel those fingertips on my skin again.

"So, tell me the rest," he said.

"The rest?"

"You said you had problems. Plural. The thieving ex is a single problem. What are the rest?"

"You really can't want to hear this," I said.

"I do. Tell me."

"Okay," I said, again unable to resist him. "But you'll be bored."

"I guarantee I won't."

Cheryl entered with a tray and set it on the table in front of us. I reached for my coffee, cradling the short, white mug in my hands, soaking in the warmth.

"The rest isn't as big a deal. My old boss, who I loved, took another position and her replacement started this week. He's -" I paused, looking for the right word. " – miserable, repellent, and lazy, to be honest with you."

"Has he been giving you trouble?" Dylan's eyes narrowed the same way they had in the bar, showing him for the predator I knew he was beneath the charm.

"Not much. Yet. But I have a bad feeling he will. He stands too close. And he's too touchy." I shuddered at the thought of those pudgy sausage fingers gripping my shoulder the way they had this morning.

"Name?" Dylan asked, pulling out his phone.

"What?"

"Give me his name. First and last. The ex as well."

"Why?"

"I'm going to check into them. The first step to dealing with a problem is information."

"You don't have to do anything about this," I said, desperately. What was going on? This was a little weird. "These are my problems. I don't expect you to get involved. It's nice enough you got me coffee and some food. You really don't need to look into Frank or Steven."

"I know I don't have to. I want to. Give me the names." His green eyes bored into me and my mouth opened involuntarily.

I gave him the names. As he typed into his phone, the door opened and a uniformed waiter pushed a cart into the room. Dylan said, "On the table, please."

Without looking at either of us, the waiter said, "Yes, sir." and began unloading the plates. As he whisked the covers off, delicious scents sent my mouth watering.

One plate held what looked like steak tartare with tiny diced onions and capers. It was one of my favorites. Another held a selection of olives and cheese with colorful pieces of bruschetta.

The last had toasted brioche rounds with crème fraiche and caviar. I hadn't had caviar in years, but the last time I had, I'd loved it. My stomach growled, and I flushed.

It always embarrassed me, feeling overweight and eating in front of people. I'd grown up with my sisters questioning every bite I put in my mouth. The idea of eating in front of

Dylan, easily the most handsome man I'd ever met, paralyzed me.

Somehow, he knew exactly what to do. Lifting a square of toast heaped with shaved beef tartare, he held it in front of my lips.

"Open," he ordered. I did. The flavor hit me first. The rich, meaty taste of the beef, the crisp bite of the capers and the pungency of the onion danced over my tongue. Then his touch settled into my consciousness.

I chewed and his fingers rested on the sensitive skin beneath my chin. He trailed one finger down my neck, stopping to slide under the wide strap of my dress, stroking my shoulder.

I'm not sure how I swallowed without choking. It was the smallest of touches, no more than a fingertip, and I was shivering, my body on sensory overload. Between my legs, the heat transmuted into a familiar moisture.

He was getting me wet just by caressing over my shoulder. Unreal.

I didn't protest when he slipped one of the caviar rounds into my mouth, this time sliding his touch along my lower lip as he pulled his hand back. My brain was firing on all the wrong cylinders.

I was ready to run, or ready to lay back and spread my legs. I made the mistake of meeting his eyes and all thought shut off. A piece of bruschetta later, Dylan handed me my coffee and sat back.

"The coffee isn't the right compliment for the flavors," he said. "But I thought you needed it more than wine."

I swallowed and managed to speak, "Thank you. The food is wonderful."

"I enjoy eating. So do my guests, so I make sure everything is top quality," he said, taking a sip of his own coffee. "Now, any other problems?"

"It's nothing worth getting into. Really." I was outright lying. My last unspoken problem felt like the biggest. It was also really embarrassing.

At least it would be, if I had to admit it to Dylan. It would be over in three days. I could get through three days.

"So there is something else. Tell me."

I resisted him this time. "No. Honestly, I'm fine. I appreciate all of this, but I don't understand why you'd help me. You just met me."

His eyes reminded me of a wolf's as they rested on my face, meeting mine, before sliding down to stroke over my body. Possessive. Confident. Predatory. I was way out of my depth.

"I want something from you," he said, bluntly. "Something only you can give me. Tell me what your last problem is, and we'll see what we can work out."

I couldn't speak. He wanted something from me? I didn't have anything. No money. Not since that bastard had cleaned me out.

And Dylan Kane could hardly need money. Ditto for accounting services. He probably had an entire floor of accountants tallying up all his cash. How could I give him anything?

"I don't -" That was as far as I got before he took my hand in his, his thumb stroking over my skin in slow swirls.

"Just tell me." His eyes bored into mine, compelling me. I wanted to tell him. However, I didn't want to see him laugh at me, either.

"I -" I stopped, not believing I was going to talk. Then my mouth opened again, and I started to speak. "I don't have a date to my sister's wedding. She's a huge bitch, and if

I show up alone, she and my other sister will make me miserable. I was supposed to go with Steven, but..."

I trailed off, unable to meet his eyes, utterly humiliated. Why had I given in? I peeked up at him, expecting to see scorn, or worse, pity. Instead, he was smiling, a wide, open smile that lit his green eyes and was oddly triumphant.

"Perfect," he said, turning my hand over in his so he could rub his thumb into my palm. "That's the easiest to solve. I'll be your date."

"What?" Not the answer I was expecting. I don't know what I thought he'd say, but it definitely wasn't that.

"I'll be your date. And in return, you'll do something for me."

"What?" I was turning into a broken record. Half-horrified and half-curious, I said, "What could you possibly want me to do for you?"

His grin deepened, turning predatory and a shade more triumphant. Still holding my hand, he reached for my arm with his free hand and tugged me closer. My body heated at his sudden proximity.

Leaning in, he whispered, "I want you in my bed. For as long as I'm your date, your body is mine. You'll give me anything I want, Leigha. And in return, I'll solve all your problems."

"I can't do that," I whispered back.

"Why not? Don't tell me you don't want to see what it would be like."

"I don't know you, and I don't have very much experience. I wouldn't know what to do."

My brain stuttered for something else to say. I couldn't do what he was suggesting. It was ridiculous. It was absolutely insane.

But it was also probably the only chance I'd ever have to

see a man like this naked. It'd be my only chance to see what sex would be like with a man who knew what he was doing.

I had no doubt that Dylan Kane was a master in bed. He'd only touched me a few times, all innocent, and I was wet and quivering. How would it feel to be the focus of all his passion, to have him order me to do something, knowing I would obey?

I felt another rush of liquid heat between my legs. I was under no illusions that this would be an equal partnership. He would be in charge. He'd own me.

Since I was old enough to think about sex, I'd had an active imagination. I'd lie in bed at night, fingers between my legs, my brain spinning fantasies of beautiful, masterful men and obedient women—sheiks and their harems, lords and serving girls.

Men like Dylan, and women who were shy and eager to please. Once I grew up and entered the real world, it was a depressing disappointment to learn that men like Dylan were rare creatures.

I'd settled for tepid, average sex, and not much of that. This might be my one chance to experience something else.

Except, the whole idea was crazy. Then, I imagined walking into the restaurant on Dylan's arm and seeing my sisters' jaws drop. Sensing my indecision, Dylan leaned in, his lips grazing the shell of my ear.

"You don't need to know what to do. I'll be in charge," he said. One hand rested on my bare knee and slid easily up my thigh, his fingers inching under the hem of my skirt.

My brain was on overdrive, afraid to say yes, afraid I'd say no. My own natural shyness combined with arousal had me frozen, unable to act.

I stuttered, "I'm not like the women here. I'm not

skinny, or -" A hard finger landed over my lips, cutting off my words.

"Don't tell me what you aren't. Don't compare yourself to other women and think you're not good enough. I know what I want. I want you. Are you saying I have bad taste?"

His question seemed absurd. Dylan Kane, have bad taste? The Delecta was known for its beautiful decor, its exquisite artwork. His casino, his office, his clothes, everything about him screamed good taste.

"No," I whispered, my lips pressed to his finger.

"Then don't insult yourself. Ever."

I nodded, my lips rubbing his skin. A devil in the back of my mind told me to reach out the tip of my tongue and taste him. He was so close. Instead, he pulled back, a thoughtful expression on his face.

"I think this would be easier for you if you had a sample. It's hard to decide when you don't know what you're getting into."

"A sample?"

"A kiss," he said.

A heartbeat later, his mouth was on mine--soft but insistent, stroking my closed lips gently before coaxing my mouth open. His hands came around my back, pulling me into his chest and pressing his body to mine.

Heat and hard muscle had my head spinning. Dylan's warm, spicy scent clouded my brain. He started slow, coaxing me with brushes of his tongue to mine, until I arched into him, eager for more.

One hand dropped to my hips, urging me to move. Before I knew it, I'd shifted to straddle his lap. The hand on my hips dragged up my skirt until my ass was bared.

His fingers sunk in, pulling me closer. The hard, thick length of his cock was between us, putting the perfect pressure on my wet pussy. My soaked panties slid against my hot flesh as I moved against him, too aroused to be self-conscious.

He fed on my mouth, his kiss no longer gentle or slow. I didn't want gentle anymore. I wanted his lips, his hands, and his cock. Arching my breasts into his chest, I moaned, lost in the sensation of his mouth on mine, his hand on my ass.

The other hand was at the zipper at the back of my dress, then at the bodice, freeing one breast. He released my mouth, pulling back enough to see me. This time, it was Dylan who moaned.

"You're perfect," he said, just before his mouth took my nipple, licking the hard tip with teasing flicks of his tongue. Sparks of heat shot through me and I felt myself moving against him and heard my moans.

Abandoning my breast, his mouth was on mine again. This time he had no need for coaxing. I was all his. I opened to him, my tongue reaching for his, rubbing and tangling with his as I panted against him.

His fingers plucked my nipple, twisting it just to the point of pain before giving it a soothing rub and cupping my breast in his hand, doing it again and again until I was mindless with pleasure.

Nothing I'd ever done with a man had felt this good, and we weren't even naked. If this went on much longer, I was going to come just from making out. I had a hard enough time coming from sex, usually.

Just kissing Dylan was miles better than my best fantasy of sex. There was no question what I would say to his proposition.

I gasped as the hand on my ass slipped inside my wet panties and stroked my pussy from behind. My entire body shuddered with need. I didn't care about modesty, didn't care about what he would think when he saw me naked.

I wanted more of that. Just as my hand dropped between us, ready to unfasten his belt, I heard the jangle of bells that signaled my phone ringing. I ignored it, stroking my fingers over the bulge of his cock through the fine wool of his suit, shaking when the back of my hand grazed my clit.

His fingertips still traced the outside of my pussy, spreading my liquid heat, driving me mindless with need.

The bells rang again. Whoever was calling wasn't going to give up. With willpower I didn't know I had, I pulled away and stumbled off Dylan's lap, reaching for my purse on the end of the couch. I answered, realizing who it had to be.

"Hello?" I said, trying to catch my breath.

"Where are you?" A shrill voice sounded in my ear. My youngest sister. The bride. And an unholy bitch most of the time. "You were supposed to meet us at the bar by the restaurant. We've been waiting for five minutes."

"Sorry," I said. "I'll be there soon."

"What are you doing? You sound like you're running. You'd better run. I can't believe you'd be late to my wedding!"

"It's not your wedding, Christie. It's just dinner. And I'll be there." I was prepared to go on, but my phone was gone.

I looked over in astonishment to see Dylan hang up on my sister and slip the phone in his suit pocket. Aside from the still visible length of his cock through his trousers, he showed no signs of what we'd been doing.

I didn't need a mirror to know my lips were swollen, my skin flushed red and my hair a mess.

"Your sister?" he asked, one brow raised. I nodded. "Is she always that unpleasant?" I nodded again. My phone began to ring.

"Do you agree to my offer?" Dylan asked. I nodded a third time.

"Yes." My voice was hoarse. "Yes, I do."

"Good." Dylan pulled my phone out of his pocket and stared at it for a moment. It continued to ring. Christie did not like being hung up on.

He slid his finger across the screen to answer the call. The sound of outraged yelling filtered from the tiny speakers. Lifting the phone to speak, he said, "We're on our way. Stop yelling at your sister."

Then he hung up again. I giggled. If our time on the couch and his way with my sister were any indication, this was going to be fun.

CHAPTER FIVE

LEIGHA

"W here are we eating?" Dylan asked, leading me to the elevator. I followed, not meeting his assistant's eyes as I tried to smooth my skirt and hair. I couldn't do anything about my pink cheeks.

"The Italian restaurant near the bar where we met. I can't remember the name."

"Passione," he said. He drew his phone from his pocket and made a call as the elevator doors slid shut. "Joe, have all the belongings in room-" Dylan turned to me, "Room number?"

"Seven eighty-five."

"Room seven eighty-five moved to my penthouse. Ask Melissa to take care of putting them away." He hung up and began tapping out a text. I stood there beside him, feeling a little foolish.

My skin still tingled, my pussy pulsed with need, and a glance in the shiny brass walls of the elevator told me it was obvious what we'd been doing. Dylan was completely fine, cool as can be, giving orders and rearranging my life to suit him—but wasn't that what I'd agreed to?

I guess it was. If we were going to be together all weekend, it made sense to share a room.

He finished his text and put the phone away, saying nothing. I shifted in my heels, the heat between my legs suddenly cold, the damp uncomfortable. Dylan stood beside me, watching the numbers change above the elevator door.

For all the attention he gave me, I might as well have been alone. Awkward didn't begin to cover it. Maybe I was making a mistake.

Not maybe. Definitely. I wasn't exactly brimming over with fantastic choices where men were concerned. Looking at it that way, what was one more? At least Dylan could kiss, which was more than I could say for some of the other men I'd chosen. Still, he was pretty much a stranger, and I'd been crawling all over him in his office.

At the thought of my eagerness, I felt my cheeks heat again. Did any other woman Dylan dated blush at the thought of making out with him? I doubted it.

Then again, we weren't really dating. When the wedding was over, I'd go back to my boring life, and I'd never see Dylan again. I might as well make the most of it.

I was so lost in my thoughts; I didn't notice the elevator had stopped until the doors slid open. Dylan's hand closed over my elbow, leading me into the main floor of the casino. I'd only arrived at the Delecta for the first time a few hours before, and I didn't have my bearings. I thought the restaurant was directly opposite the elevators we'd used.

At first, that's where Dylan led me. Then he veered abruptly to our right, pulling me down a long row of flashing slot machines, past a bar, behind a potted palm tree and halfway down a dim, carpeted hallway. He stopped exactly between two nondescript metal doors, completely out of sight of the busy casino floor.

What were we doing back here? My brain couldn't catch up. Dylan's long body pressed close, pinning me to the wall. His leg pushed between mine, spreading my thighs and sliding my skirt up my legs.

I opened my mouth to speak, and he covered it with his, his tongue sliding between my open lips, his breath hot on my skin. Just like that, the heat was back.

One hand found the hem of my dress, inching it upwards, reaching around to squeeze my ass before slipping between my legs, into my panties. At the graze of his fingertips along my still wet pussy, I moaned into his mouth.

"Shhh," he said, breaking our kiss. "No camera here. Not if we don't move. But you don't want anyone to hear you, to come see us, do you?"

I moaned again. I didn't. I really didn't. Did I? No. Now that he'd said something, though, I thought I felt eyes out there, crawling over us. Watching. I shivered, partly from the thought of a stranger watching us kiss, seeing Dylan's hand up my dress.

His hand was doing more than coasting along my fevered skin. He dipped two fingertips inside, soaking them in my aroused heat before pulling them back and circling my clit. More shivers. His touch was light, teasing me with pleasure, but it sent sparks of need through every cell. I ached to move, to moan and beg.

Dimly aware that we were only a few yards from the bustling floor of the casino, I did my best to stay still and silent. Tiny whimpers spilled from my lips.

"Shhh. This will have to be quick," Dylan breathed into

my ear. "I thought I could wait until after dinner, but I can't. I want to see you come now."

He pushed two long fingers deep into my wet pussy in one hard thrust, stretching me in a brilliant flare of pleasure. His two fingers were bigger than any cock I'd taken before. He would split me open when he finally got inside me. I'd felt him when we were kissing before. Sex with Dylan would be in a class by itself.

Just this, his fingers inside me, the heel of his palm grinding my clit as I thrust my hips against him, was the best sex I'd ever had and it wasn't even sex.

The orgasm hit me in a rush, splintering through me as he muffled my moans with his mouth. He played with me, thrusting his fingers, circling his palm on my clit, drawing it out until my knees wobbled and my moans faded into panting breaths.

I'd never come that fast in my life. Granted, I'd been primed from our kiss in his office, but an orgasm was never a guarantee for me, even when I was alone. Every muscle in my legs shook, and I was glad the wall was there to hold me up.

His hard cock pressed into my hip, reminding me that I'd been completely passive, allowing him to do as he pleased, but offering nothing back. Before I could think better of it, I sank to my knees, reaching for his belt.

Dylan's fingers slipped from between my legs. He touched my face with his other hand. Maybe he wanted to stop me. I didn't care. I knew I was supposed to let him lead, but I wanted to give him something back. I wanted his cock.

His fingers had been amazing. Fantastic. Better than I could have imagined. But I wanted to touch him. I wanted him in my mouth.

My fingers fumbled as I opened his belt. I ignored the

whisper of my name above me, pushed away the faint sounds of the slot machines filtering down the hall. His hard length pressed against his zipper, waiting for me to release him.

I had to be fast. We'd only been in there for a few minutes, but I had no idea if anyone would be coming, or if the doors on either side of us led anywhere. Maybe they'd open and people would come streaming out. Just the thought spurred me to get on with it. I'd have plenty of time to linger over his cock later. For now, I needed to stay focused.

He was too big for me to take all of him in my mouth. I wasn't exactly the queen of blow jobs. I'd given a few. Mainly to boyfriends, of which there hadn't been many. It had been a while since I'd been here, kneeling before a man, my hand on him, lips open and eager.

Actually, my lips had never been eager. And I'd never thought of it as a 'cock'. Always a penis if I mentally used a word for it at all. What I had before me was a cock. Thick and long, this was the tool of a man, not a boy.

I circled my hand around his girth, unable to close my fingers. I whimpered at the thought of taking him between my legs. The pressure. I'd be so full. I licked his head, tasting the drop of moisture at the tip. Musky and male.

I wanted more. Using my hand to stroke where my mouth couldn't reach, I dropped my jaw and took as much of him as I could. Above me, I heard a low groan.

I moaned in response, the vibration teasing him as I sucked and licked, my hand stroking in the same rhythm. With my other hand, I cupped his balls, pressing two fingers into his perineum. He thrust back at me, driving his cock deeper into my mouth, hitting the back of my throat.

I choked for a second before I relaxed. With any other

man, that would have been it. I would have pushed him back, overwhelmed. But I'd never wanted a cock like this before. I wanted him in my mouth, wanted his taste, wanted to feel him come and know I'd given that to him.

Breathing through my nose, I tried to relax and let him thrust, twisting my hand, sucking in hard pulls. I stroked my tongue around the head of his cock when he drew back, tasting every inch of him. My pussy, so recently satisfied, pulsed between my legs, jealous of my mouth. It wanted him to fuck between my legs instead of my lips.

I was happy exactly where I was, inhaling his scent, feeling the need build in his jagged thrusts. His balls pulled tight to his body, and I sucked harder, not letting myself ease back as he buried his cock in the opening of my throat and came, groaning my name into the empty hall.

I sucked out the last of his orgasm, reveling in the taste of his come. Another first. I'd swallowed before, but never because I really wanted to. This time, I'd needed it, needed to feel his pleasure inside me. Fingertips caressed the side of my face with a touch that was almost sweet.

Then his hands were under my arms and I was on my feet, shoved back into the wall, his mouth on mine, my body pressed to the length of his. When he broke away, we were both panting. He stepped back and busied himself straightening his clothes. I looked down, suddenly shy, wiping the backs of my fingers across my mouth.

I had a sudden wish for lipstick, or at least some gloss. Something that might shield my mouth from others, a cosmetic armor against anyone realizing what I'd just done.

Unfortunately, I'd brought a tiny purse that held nothing more than my phone, my ID and a debit card. I hadn't thought to add any makeup, not even lip gloss. I'd have to brazen it out. It wasn't like I'd done anything wrong, anyway.

Finished with his belt, Dylan took my elbow once more, leading me back into the crowded casino floor. I managed to keep up without tripping over my heels, my head spinning. It went without saying that I'd never done anything like that before.

No one had seen us, so it wasn't exactly public sex, but it was closer than I'd ever come. The idea that Dylan had wanted me so badly sent tingles down my spine. Me, plump, boring, Leigha Carmichael had somehow managed to interest a man like Dylan Kane. I couldn't quite take it in.

Up ahead, through the crowd, I spotted my family waiting for me. Taking a deep breath, I told myself to get it together. Facing my sisters with my head in the clouds was a bad idea. They could eat me alive when I was on guard. Distracted, they'd pull me apart in seconds.

CHAPTER SIX

DYLAN

She was completely unexpected. When I saw her in the bar, I was drawn by her abundant curves - those ripe tits and her round ass pushing the seams of her conservative dress to its limits.

Then we met, and her sweet, shy demeanor was its own hook, as were her pretty face and her clear grey eyes. Instead of jumping on my offer of help, she'd pushed me away. It wasn't my power that made her melt, it was my body. One kiss and she'd been creaming all over me.

I knew women found me attractive. They'd been after me since I hit my first growth spurt at fourteen. As I'd grown older, and more visibly successful, it got harder to tell what they wanted more, me or what was in my bank account.

Not Leigha. Unless she was an exceptional actress, news of my wealth and position had only made her more nervous. Until I got my hands on her, that is. Then she'd gone wild. That kiss was insane.

One touch of my lips and she'd opened for me, her

tongue reaching for mine, letting me guide her onto my lap, not even flinching when my hand slid under her skirt. If her sister hadn't called, I'd have been fucking that sweet, tight pussy a minute after getting my hands on her ass.

And her tits were exceptional. I couldn't even think about those without getting fully hard and I'd only just come in her mouth. Jesus, let's not forget about that mouth.

I'd dragged her into the hallway, grateful I knew the exact spot where the cameras didn't overlap, because I couldn't wait a second longer to get my fingers inside her.

My cock would have been better, but there hadn't been time for that. She'd been soaked, like a hot, wet vice. So tight, she must have had all pencil-dicked boyfriends. She'd gone off like a rocket, her face an arousing combination of surprise and ecstasy.

But the blow job was what got me. Not just that it was good, or that she'd let me in her throat, both surprises in themselves. No, it was her hunger. Her need to get her mouth on me. She didn't hit her knees because she felt she had to, or thought she should.

She'd sucked me like she loved my cock. Like she couldn't get enough, and could have sucked me all day. She'd swallowed my come without a flinch. I'd had women do that before, either because they loved to suck cock or they knew how to fake it. But never one this clean. This innocent.

Leigha was a revelation. One I was finding I wanted more than I'd expected.

We had to get through this dinner with her family. Then I was taking her to my penthouse. I might not let her out all weekend, except for the wedding.

If fucking her was anything like having her suck me off, she was going to have a hard time walking by Sunday night.

CHAPTER SEVEN

LEIGHA

I found myself leaning into Dylan as we approached my mother, sisters, and Peter, my future brother in law. Three (bleached) blond heads turned in our direction at Peter's nudge.

Then three jaws dropped. I'd be lying if I said I didn't get some well-deserved satisfaction out of that. The three of them had always been peas in a pod–outgoing, pretty, popular, and skinny.

A constant stream of boyfriends rang our doorbell when I was in high school, all for Cathie, Christie and my mom. Only a few for me, and those never lasted long. Not once one of my vivacious sisters decided to steal him away.

They didn't actually like my dates; they just thought it was funny to see how quickly they'd dump me for the promise of a popular girl guaranteed to put out.

I was the only female in my house who'd gone to college to get an education. While I'd graduated with a degree in business and accounting, then gone for my CPA, Christie and Cathie had been trying to figure out the best way to get an engagement ring before junior year.

Now, only a few years after they would have graduated, they both had a marriage and a divorce on their résumés. There was no actual employment unless you count the arduous task of interviewing housekeepers and divorce lawyers.

We were here at the Delecta so Christie could rope Peter and make him her latest sucker. I didn't feel sorry for him. He was handsome, successful, and a complete asshole. As far as I was concerned, they deserved each other.

Dylan's arm around my waist pulled me closer, tucking me into his side as we stopped before my family. Before they could speak, he said,

"I apologize for our lateness, it was my fault. I'm Dylan Kane." He held out his hand to my mother, who took it, her jaw still half dropped.

"Not *THE* Dylan Kane?" she asked, breathlessly. I braced for the embarrassment to come. As I expected, she moved in, sidling closer so she could lay an overly familiar hand on the lapel of Dylan's suit. "The owner of all of this? Girls, you know who Dylan Kane is!"

Before she could get any closer, Dylan eased back, stepping slightly behind me while keeping his arm firmly around my waist. "It's a pleasure to meet you, Mrs. Carmichael," Dylan said, polite in the face of her attempted groping.

Not one to give up easily, my mother giggled, a young, high-pitched sound I'd always hated. It usually meant she was up to something.

"Oh, I'm not Mrs. Carmichael. That was the girls' father's name. I've moved on since then. I'm Mrs. Lowe, but you can call me Barbara."

Unable to help myself, I went to my toes and whispered in Dylan's ear, "The Mrs. Lowe is from husband number four."

"Are you going to introduce me to your sisters?" he whispered back, his breath tickling my ear. I caught Christie scowling at me. She was justified. Whispering in front of all of them was kind of rude, but I couldn't bring myself to feel badly about it.

"Only if you promise not to sleep with any of them," I said into the side of his neck, my voice so low I knew he could barely hear. In response, I got another squeeze of his arm, followed by a light kiss to my temple.

"This is Cathie, Christie, and Christie's fiancé, Peter," I said, gesturing to each of them in turn.

"Nice to meet you," Dylan said, then turned to the restaurant. "Do we have a reservation? I know it's my fault we're late, and I'd hate for everyone to go hungry."

My mother finally remembered why we were there and led us to the hostess stand. A moment later, we were on our way to our table, a large circular booth surrounded by light drapes suspended from the ceiling. The design of the restaurant was intimate and cozy. Wonderful for a date, not so fabulous for a family dinner.

As we arranged ourselves in the booth, Cathie gave me a hip bump designed to send me reeling into Peter, giving her room to sit beside Dylan. Dylan refused to release his hold on my waist, and instead of letting me fall, he used my sideways momentum to slide me into the booth, with him beside me.

Smooth. And sweet. Unfortunately, I ended up with Peter on my other side. Unable to finagle a seat next to Dylan, who'd taken the end of the booth, Cathie slid in on the other end and glared at me.

"So, what are you doing with Leigha?" she asked, venom dripping from her words. "You're not actually her date, are you? She works for you or something, right?"

"I work at Haywood and Cross, Cathie," I said, cutting in. "I've been there since I graduated from college."

"And Leigha is most definitely my date," Dylan said. "I'd love to get her working for me, but Haywood and Cross is a great firm. I doubt I could entice her away. And it would interfere with our," he paused and met my eyes, "*personal* relationship."

Across the booth I heard Cathie whisper to Christie, "I think I just threw up a little. Tell me he's not sleeping with her. So gross." I flushed in embarrassment. If I'd heard, so had the rest of the table. They weren't exactly subtle.

"How did you two meet?" my mother asked, covering the awkward silence left after Cathie's comment.

"As so often happens in a town like this," Dylan said, "We met at a bar. I saw Leigha across the room and I knew I had to get to know her better." He smiled down at me, his expression the perfect representation of a doting boyfriend. He was good. If I wasn't careful I'd find myself believing it.

"And you asked her out?" Christie said.

"Of course."

"But she's fat." This from Christie. My mother murmured her name in an embarrassed protest.

"And boring," Cathie added. "She's an accountant for God's sake. How much more boring does it get?"

Christie leaned around my mother to meet Cathie's eyes. "Do you remember the boys she dated when we were in high-school?"

"Oh my God, such losers. Remember the one from the math club? They did that thing together?"

"He was such a dork," Christie said, her giggle a replica

38

of my mother's. My mother rolled her eyes at us in a half-hearted apology.

"Girls, don't be rude. Maybe if you two had spent a little more time in the math club and less time on dates, you would have graduated with a 4.0 like your sister. And that thing she and the boy from math club did was a very complicated project. They won some kind of prize for it, didn't you honey?"

"We worked with the robotics club on navigational calculations for a drone they built. We won a grant for the school with it."

"Impressive," Dylan said, giving me that intimate boyfriend smile again. I couldn't help melting a little, especially when he followed up by squeezing my knee under the table. His fingertips traced my kneecap in slow, deliberate circles, distracting me from the conversation.

"It was the only way she could get a date," Cathie cut in. "Fishing at the bottom of the barrel."

"It didn't stop you from sleeping with him," I said, sweetly. Maybe she'd been more popular than me, but most of that was because she slept around. A lot. Not just *'healthy young woman with an active sex drive'* a lot but *'trying to get attention any way I can'* a lot.

"Someone had to," she shot back, not ashamed. "God knows you weren't going to."

"Leave your sister alone," my mother said to them. "It wasn't her fault she was overweight and shy." Turning to Dylan, she went on, "Leigha was always a good girl. Bright. Well behaved. Never gave me a second of trouble. Not like these two."

That was the reason I was even there. While my sisters were turbo bitches most of the time, my mom meant well. She got married way too often and was always on the prowl for her next husband, but she loved me and she showed it as best she could.

When I'd tried to beg off the wedding, even though it was only a few miles from my house, she'd said, "But I never see you anymore. I miss you!" I'd been helpless to say no.

At that moment, I fiercely regretted not sticking to my guns, even if being there had put me in Dylan's path. Sitting through dinner with those two was going to kill me with humiliation.

I knew I'd wake up that night, or sometime next week, with the perfect comebacks echoing in my head. I always thought of them later, never on the spot. Under the glare of their cutting comments, my throat would swell shut and I could never think of anything good to say. Accusing Cathie of sleeping around didn't count since she considered it a badge of honor.

The waitress interrupted with our menus and a recitation of the specials. I was still starving, despite the appetizers Dylan had fed me in his office. The next few minutes were occupied with deciding what to order, my sisters saying I should I get a side salad to keep my calories down, and Dylan suggesting the lasagna or the linguine pescatore.

When Christie gasped in horror and said, "Girls like Leigha can't eat pasta. Too many carbs." Dylan skewered her with a look and murmured in my ear, loud enough for the table to hear,

"I love to watch you eat, don't I?" Then he pressed a kiss to my mouth.

I felt my skin turn a bright, hot red. His hand left off tracing circles on my knee and slid up to the middle of my leg, the weight of his palm heavy, a claiming, while his fingertips teased the sensitive skin of my inner thigh. My pussy, so close to his touch, heated. Again.

"Shall I order for you?" he asked. I nodded, mouth dry.

I looked around the table, trying to pretend Dylan didn't have his hand between my legs under the table. My mother was smiling at us. Christie and Cathie scowled in confusion. And Peter studied me with a curious, appraising look, as if Dylan's interest was making him wonder what I might have to offer.

Yuck. He was a perfect match for my sister, with his overly polished good looks and the bank account to match her desire to never work a day in her life. But when you scratched the surface, he was all asshole.

A few months before, at a dinner to celebrate their engagement, I'd caught him berating the valet driver over a nonexistent scratch on his sports car. This was after he treated our waiter with rude dismissal and then tipped him less than five percent. Not to mention that he'd grabbed my butt on the way out of the restaurant. I'd whirled and hit him on the arm. He'd backed off, but the whole thing made me uncomfortable.

Resolving to ignore him, I turned my attention back to Dylan, whose fingers were slowly inching their way up my thigh. He wouldn't actually touch me at the table, would he?

Taking in the amused, aroused glimmer in his eyes, I realized that he would, if he wanted to. I just had to hope he didn't want to. All it took was the memory of what those fingers had done and my body was ready for more.

I zoned out, barely listening to my sisters chatter on about the wedding, something about the flowers, or the place settings, all my attention focused on Dylan and his roving fingers. His right foot hooked my left and tugged, spreading my legs just enough to make room for his hand. I hitched a breath as his thumb skated across my clit.

"What's wrong with you?" Cathie asked. I shook my head, and grabbed Dylan's hand under the table, desperate to stop him before I embarrassed myself.

"Nothing," I said. "I'm fine."

"Your face looks weird," she said, wrinkling her nose at me.

I didn't care; I was more worried that Dylan was going to make me come right there at the table. I knew he could. If what had happened in the hallway was any indication, he could do it before our entrees arrived with time to spare.

"Stop," I breathed into Dylan's ear. He shook his head in a barely perceptible movement. Leaning in, he said, so quietly I could only hear a thread of sound,

"You're going to come. Do you want it here, or upstairs?"

"Upstairs. Please upstairs."

"What are you two whispering about again?" Christie asked, looking annoyed that we weren't paying attention to her story about where she'd found her bridesmaid dresses. Dylan straightened, drawing his hand back into his own lap.

"I apologize, that was rude of us. I was just telling Leigha that an urgent message came in on my phone and we're going to have to excuse ourselves."

"Oh, can't Leigha stay?" my mother asked, the only one who cared if I was there or not. I felt a little bad about letting her down, but not enough to stay. Especially not if Dylan was taking me upstairs to give me an orgasm.

"I'm sorry, we have a commitment after this, so she'll have to come with me. As an apology, dinner is on me. We'll see you tomorrow. It was a pleasure meeting all of you."

With a nod, he pulled me from the booth and we were on our way out of the restaurant. Dylan stopped at the hostess station to say,

"Put their dinner on my account, Melanie. And send them a bottle of the Perrier-Jouët 2006 Belle Epoque Brut. Have our meals sent upstairs along with a piece of the mascarpone chocolate cheesecake."

"Yes, sir. Office or penthouse?"

"Penthouse."

CHAPTER EIGHT

LEIGHA

We rode the elevator in silence, standing side-by-side, not touching. The lack of contact was excruciating. After sitting so close in the restaurant with his arm around me and then his hand on my leg, the space between us made me feel alone.

And nervous.

I was pretty sure he hadn't changed his mind. But what if he had? Halfway through the ride, I couldn't take the quiet anymore.

"I'm sorry about my sisters. And my mom kind of hitting on you." I didn't know what else to say. They were rude, and it was embarrassing. Dylan looked at me, his eyes impossible to read.

"Your mother was fine. Your sisters are atrocious. Did they really steal your boyfriends in high school?"

"There weren't that many," I said. "But, yeah. They didn't want to go out with the guys. They just wanted to, I don't know, humiliate me? Show me what a dork I was? I was in the math club and the chess club so it's not like I didn't already know."

Dylan gave me another long, unreadable look. I forced myself not to squirm, or tug at the hem of my skirt.

"They're bitches, Leigha. They'll probably always be bitches. Don't let them bother you."

"I try not to. Mostly, I avoid them."

"Good." Dylan turned his attention back to the elevator doors, making me even more edgy. Finally, the elevator stopped at a floor marked P*. Taking my arm, Dylan led me into a luxurious entryway complete with a crystal chandelier and polished parquet floors.

Opposite the elevator hung an oil painting that made me wish I knew more about art. It was certainly original and undoubtedly expensive. Below the painting, a wide, decorative China bowl sat between two fresh flower arrangements on an antique sideboard.

Tall, wide double doors flanked the entryway. In contrast to the casino's more modern decor, it was like entering another world.

Dylan punched in a code on the doors to our right. Inside, it was more of the same. Polished parquet in a warm, honey-toned wood, covered by Oriental rugs. More oil paintings hung on the walls. Antiques were everywhere.

The space was masculine, yet welcoming. The furniture was large enough to accommodate a man of Dylan's height, but not bulky. I followed Dylan into what appeared to be the main living room, trying to take it all in without looking like I was overwhelmed by the opulence.

He stopped in the middle of the room, between a long brown leather sofa and gas fireplace surrounded by a hand carved mantle that would have been at home in an English gentleman's club.

"Take off your dress."

My brain stuttered as my body flared with arousal. I was still turned on from his teasing in the restaurant, but the elevator ride had given me time to cool off just enough for insecurity to creep back in. Take off my dress in the middle of the living room? I couldn't do that. It was too exposed.

One look at Dylan's face told me I didn't have a choice. I'd made a deal - he was my date, and I gave him what he wanted. Maybe I should've thought that last part through a little more carefully before I'd agreed.

"Are you going to make me wait?"

Dylan raised one eyebrow and stared me down. There was just enough threat implied in his question that I wasn't eager to see what would happen if I disobeyed for much longer.

I shook my head. No, I wasn't going to make him wait.

I might pass out from the combination of arousal and embarrassed terror, but I'd take off the damn dress.

It took a little squirming to reach the zipper between my shoulder blades and pull it down. The fabric was stretched tight around my torso, strained by my breasts and my not-so-svelte figure.

I couldn't look Dylan in the eyes as I tugged at it. When I got it past my rib cage, it slid the rest of the way freely and the dress fell to the floor, pooling around my feet.

Dylan paced around me, his eyes soaking in every inch of my half naked body, standing there in black spike heels and mismatched bra and underwear.

At least the underwear was nice. The thought that I might have been wearing laundry day panties was too hideous to consider.

My navy lace boy shorts and black lace bra weren't new, but at least they were presentable and looked decent on my curvy body. I waited, trembling a little from the tension, wondering what he would say next. I didn't have to wait long.

"Now the bra. Straps first."

I reached up and hooked a finger through my left bra strap. The bra I was wearing was intended for containment. It needed those straps. Without them it wouldn't cover me for long.

Finding the courage to meet Dylan's eyes, I drew down the first strap and let it fall limp against my arm. As I'd known it would, the lace on that side of the bra began to slide, exposing the upper swell of my cleavage, until it hung on the tip of my hard nipple.

Dylan's eyes flared with heat.

Encouraged, I drew down the other strap and let the bra fall away. He stood three feet from me, but his gaze felt like a touch, insistent and demanding.

My insecurity drained away. I reached behind me with one hand and flicked the clasp on the bra, letting it fall to the floor. My breasts swelled under his attention, begging for his hands or his mouth.

"Panties. Off," he ordered, his voice low, gruff.

I obeyed, sliding my palms flat down the sides of my hips, pushing the boy shorts along with them until they fell around my feet with my dress.

Normally, the thought of being stark naked in front of anyone--especially a man as beautiful as Dylan--would have had me hyperventilating with panic, searching for the closest dark room.

The arousal on his face was enough to keep me where I was. Whatever I saw when I looked in the mirror, Dylan saw something different. Something he wanted.

He reached out a hand. Taking an unsteady step forward, I slid my fingers into his.

Silent, he led me across the room to the tall windows overlooking the garish lights of Vegas.

He raised one of my hands and placed it against the glass, forcing me to bend forward slightly. He positioned my other hand beside it, so my hands were just wider than shoulder width apart.

"Don't move until I tell you to," he said. "Don't turn your head and don't close your eyes."

Then he stepped away, and I was alone, unable to see what he was doing.

I trembled in my heels, my palms leaving damp marks on the glass, my breath creating a circle of mist in front of my face. I needed him to do something. I needed him to touch me.

To fuck me.

To do anything.

Behind me, I heard a knock at the door. Instinctively, I began to turn my head, only to hear,

"No."

A flat command. One I obeyed instantly.

Trembling harder, I stared blindly out into the night, not seeing the lights of the strip, catching only vague shadows of movement in the reflection of the window in front of me.

"Put it over there please," I heard Dylan say. Then the sound of rolling wheels.

Our food. I'd completely forgotten about the dinner we hadn't eaten. And now the waiter could see me, completely naked.

I was grateful Dylan had told me not to look. If I'd seen the waiter's face, and he'd seen mine, this would've been humiliating. As it was, he could only see the backside of my body.

I was somewhat obscured in the dim room and mostly anonymous.

To my surprise, a second set of eyes only made me hotter. I could feel the molten heat of my pussy, the moisture gathering so quickly I thought it might begin to run down my inner thighs.

How long would Dylan make me wait?

Was the waiter going to stay? I hoped not. As arousing as it was to be on display like this, Dylan on his own was more than I could handle. Throwing a stranger into the mix would be way too much.

I heard a few murmured words and the sound of the door shutting. Then one set of footsteps coming in my direction. I was pretty sure the waiter was gone.

Dylan moved so quietly, I didn't know he was behind me until I felt the tip of one long finger trace the lips of my swollen pussy. Without thought, I surged back, wanting more of him. The finger disappeared.

"Don't move."

I obeyed, too desperate for his touch to think about defying him. It would be no hardship for Dylan to find another woman to satisfy him if I couldn't do what I was told. But I didn't want another man, I wanted him—and to have him, I would have to be obedient.

Submissive.

I'd never thought about playing this kind of game before in real life, never imagined it would get me so hot outside of my fantasies.

But then, it wouldn't have if I'd been with anyone else. I knew that. Of all the men I'd known, only Dylan had ever made me mindless with arousal. I fought to control my shaking, to keep completely still.

A moment later I was rewarded by the touch of his hand to my hip.

Then, I felt the length of his body against my back, still clothed in his suit, as he pressed forward and filled his hands with my breasts. He kneaded them, stroking and pinching my nipples, twisting them back and forth until tears of frustrated arousal ran from the corners of my eyes.

"These are perfect," he whispered in my ear. "You have perfect breasts." I moaned, almost sobbing with need.

"Please. Please." I didn't even know where the words were coming from; some deep part of myself wanted more than the tepid orgasms I'd had before I'd met Dylan. I wanted this-the intensity, the rich, luscious pleasure of having him touch me.

Still, I needed more. I needed his cock. I needed him to fuck me.

"Is this what you want?"

Hot, hard, velvet skin brushed against my inner thigh just below the curve of my ass, leaving a streak of moisture behind.

"Yes," I breathed. "Yes, please. Please, Dylan."

The head of his cock homed in on my pussy, nudging into my heat, teasing me. I was so wet, he didn't have to take it slowly. But he did, easing his way in with subtle, rocking thrusts that filled me so gradually I was incoherent with need by the time he filled me to the root.

He stayed there, unmoving except to brace one hand on the window beside mine, his cock stretching me almost to the point of pain. Somehow, I managed to fight my instincts to move against him.

He must have known what a struggle it was, because he

dipped his head to mine and said, "Good girl. Now you get your reward."

His strong white teeth bit the shell of my ear, the tiny flash of pain welcome in the midst of so much pleasure.

His free hand closed over my breast, squeezing and teasing my hard nipple, sending shooting sparks straight to my clit. When he began to thrust, I think I screamed from the glory of it.

I forgot all about being shy, or quiet, or still. I moved against him, arching my lower back to take as much of his cock as I could, moaning and crying out from the sheer liquid ecstasy of his length splitting me open.

Dimly, I heard Dylan let out his own groans behind me. My orgasm had been building for so long I didn't realize how close it was until it hit.

Every touch, every tease since the restaurant had layered on top of one another until I was drowning in my own hyper-aroused body.

It seemed like only a few breaths between when he entered me and when I came, my pussy clenching down on his cock so hard it hurt, screams torn from my chest, my release so strong I almost blacked out.

My limbs went weak; the only things holding me up were Dylan's hand on my breast, my palms against the glass, and his hard cock inside me. I was still coming, my pussy pulsing around him, my hips rolling in involuntary thrusts.

Dylan's teeth locked onto the side of my neck in a grip of possession as he pounded out his own orgasm, filling me with his release.

CHAPTER NINE

DYLAN

She was a revelation. The entire night hadn't been what I'd expected. I pulled out of Leigha's clinging pussy and stepped back, taking in the sight of her lush, curvy body, damp with perspiration, flushed with passion, our come dripping down the insides of her thighs.

She was innocence debauched, her dark hair tousled, her eyes still closed, those pink lips parted as she gasped for air. I'd known she would be good. That was why I'd suffered through a half an hour with her ridiculous family. I'd had no idea she would be this good.

Leigha was gorgeous. She was a real woman, beautiful, with real curves and real responses. Her soft, heavy breasts were a dream all on their own. Add in that tight, eager pussy, and she was perfect. Her intelligence and sweetness were only a bonus.

Whatever I'd thought I was getting myself into when I'd proposed being her date in exchange for her body, things had changed.

She thought this was just for a weekend. She thought I would let her walk away. Before the next two days were over, Leigha Carmichael would learn. She was mine, for as long as I wanted her.

CHAPTER TEN

LEIGHA

I woke up to the sound of the door closing, the metallic click startling me out of my dreams. For a second, I didn't know where I was. The room was dark, the bed wide, the sheets heavy and silky smooth. It wasn't my bedroom, I knew that much.

I'd been living there for two years, and still hadn't hung curtains to block the early morning sun. My bed was a double with the same sheets I'd had in college.

Stroking a hand over the fabric covering my naked body, I resolved to get a new set of sheets at home ASAP. I didn't want to think about what they'd cost, but Dylan's sheets were amazing.

Dylan. The thought of his name brought the night before rushing back. First, meeting him in the bar, making that insane deal, then sucking his cock in a hallway, almost in plain view of the whole casino.

And the orgasms. I'd never had sex like that before. I never even imagined I would. Leaning up against the window in his living room, my eyes on the lights of Vegas as he fucked me from behind was unbelievable.

Sitting up in the bed, I pulled the sheet around me and looked for Dylan. The room was empty, the bathroom door wide open, and the light off.

From what I'd seen the night before, the penthouse was enormous, so he might be somewhere else, but he wasn't in the master suite.

There was a folded note on the bedside table. It read, *At the gym, back by 9:30.* A glance at the clock told me I had an hour before he was back. Part of me wanted to laze around in bed, but the rest of me desperately wanted a shower.

Getting up, I headed for the bathroom to see my toiletries arranged neatly on the right side of the sink. If I had to guess, I'd bet my clothes were hung equally neatly in the closet.

It must be nice to have a whole hotel's worth of employees ready to jump to do your bidding.

I'd never aspired to wealth. I'd always just wanted to be secure - a good job, with a decent place to live, and maybe enough money to go on vacation occasionally.

But it was fun to see what the other side was like even if it was only for a few days, though.

I could happily start with the bathroom. Easily bigger than my living room at home, it had a wide, creamy, marble counter, with a square custom designed sink set in the middle.

The mirror was huge, framed in gilt, the linens all top quality.

The shower and tub were opposite the sink, and both were big enough for an orgy. I couldn't guess how much water it would take to fill the tub, though I'd love to find out.

Fashioned from the same creamy marble as the rest of

the bathroom, it sat beside the shower, in front of yet another window overlooking Vegas. It looked more like a hand carved piece of sculpture than a bathtub.

As much as I would have loved to try it out, I headed for the oversized shower instead. A quick look in the mirror showed ratty hair, eyeliner circles under my eyes and pillow creases on my cheek.

I didn't want Dylan to see me like this. Not if I could help it.

It took me a minute to figure out the controls for the multiple showerheads, but once I got it, I started to think about redoing my whole bathroom at home. His shower was amazing - jets of water coming from all sides as a waterfall spilled from above. Yum.

Then I remembered Steven and my empty bank account.

Never mind. No new bathroom for me. Not for a long time. And probably no new sheets either.

I pushed that problem to the back of my mind. There was nothing I could do about Steven and all the money he'd stolen, so there was no point in dwelling on it.

When would I get another chance to spend the weekend with a hot billionaire who was fantastic in bed? Likely, this was my one and only shot, so I wasn't going to waste it moping about my asshole ex and his theft of my life savings.

Instead, I'd think about the night before.

The sex alone was enough to keep my brain occupied. The way he'd taken me against the glass window, not letting me turn to look at him, was beyond hot.

And after, when I'd finally gotten my breath back, he'd wrapped me in a loosely woven blanket and led me to the couch where he'd fed me bites of the meals we'd abandoned when we'd fled the dinner with my family.

I vaguely remembered Dylan letting the waiter in while I'd stood at the window, naked and under orders not to move. At the time it made me hot.

I should have been embarrassed about it, now that I'd had a night to sleep on it and I wasn't so turned on. But I wasn't embarrassed.

I wasn't sure why. Maybe because I'd been following Dylan's orders. There was something both freeing and arousing about giving him responsibility for my decisions.

I'd always been the responsible one, the one who had the bills paid on time, was never late, and took care of everyone else.

Now that I was an adult and living on my own, I only had myself to care for, but my job involved making the best decisions I could for others--decisions that could cost them a lot of money if my judgement was off.

Letting Dylan take over, if just for a little while, had felt like freedom. It was only playing, only sex--Not real life. That made it even better.

He'd taken me to bed after the last bite of the decadent cheesecake he'd ordered, sliding into those smooth sheets bedside me before turning my naked body to his and making love to me all over again.

I didn't remember falling asleep, just those last moments of laying on top of him, his cock still inside me as his hands roamed up and down my back. We had a whole day to kill before the rehearsal dinner.

I wondered what he had planned.

CHAPTER ELEVEN

DYLAN

I ended my work out early. I never did that. It was the one part of my day I kept for myself, no matter what else was going on with the casino and Kane Enterprises. But that morning, I couldn't get Leigha off my mind.

Running on the treadmill, then lifting weights, all I could think about was her—naked, sleeping in my bed, waiting for me to come back and fuck her again. Just the thought of her tight, hot pussy and those full tits had me half hard.

Not exactly what I was going for when I was surrounded by a room full of sweaty strangers. Fuck the workout.

I could get a different kind of workout upstairs.

I heard the shower as soon as I opened the bedroom door. At the mental image of Leigha slick with soap, my cock went from half hard to a steel bar. I hoped she was ready for me.

I'd come inside her three times the day before and it still hadn't been enough.

Opening the bathroom door slowly, so she wouldn't see me right away, I watched her through the film of steam on the glass shower doors.

Her head was tipped back as she rinsed her hair, pink lips parted, upper back arched just enough to point her heavy breasts up toward the ceiling. I couldn't wait another second.

Stripping off my workout clothes, I paced to the shower and pulled open the door, enjoying her squeal of surprise.

"What are you doing here?" she asked, eyes wide. I nudged her out of the stream of water and tipped my own head back, rinsing away the sweat from my workout.

"I live here."

"I thought you wouldn't be back until later. You surprised me."

"A good surprise or a bad surprise?" I asked, watching her pupils dilate as she took in my already hard cock. For a moment, she said nothing, but looked her fill.

"A very good surprise," she said, reaching for the bottle of soap on the shelf. "Turn around," she whispered.

So far I'd been the one in control of everything between us.

The only thing Leigha had done on her own was that blowjob in the hall the night before. Given how fucking amazing that had been, I was more than happy to let her take over, at least for now. She didn't disappoint.

Filling her hands with soap, she ran them over my back, slicking the suds over my skin, massaging and stroking me clean.

She didn't rush, taking her time to explore every inch of my back before she moved on to my arms.

I thought she'd turn me around before she went any lower, but she squeezed out more soap and dropped to her knees, smoothing her hands over my ass before giving me a tight squeeze. Then down to my hamstrings and my calves.

My cock was so hard, I was leaking drops of pre-come. It took everything I had to resist taking charge. But I wanted to see how far Leigha would go.

Finally, she stood and moved around my body, facing me. She met my eyes, her grey gaze an intoxicating swirl of lust and nerves.

Her natural shyness, combined with her lush body and her uninhibited sexual response, had me hooked. The more I had of her, the more I wanted.

She didn't really fit my life, but I didn't care.

I was Dylan Kane.

I could make her fit if I wanted to.

Stroking her hands across my shoulders, she spread the slippery soap over my skin, rubbing lightly, as if focused on actually getting me clean. Then she did something that surprised me.

She tipped the bottle of soap over her chest and rubbed it in until her full, round breasts shone with gleaming bubbles. Leaning closer, she pressed herself to my chest and shifted her skin back and forth against mine, using her tits to clean me.

The sensation was mind blowing. I was already in love with her breasts, their weight and fullness, the way they spilled over my hands. But, having them stroking me, slipping over my chest, hard nipples almost digging in as she moved herself in circles on my skin, made this the best shower of my life.

I didn't know how much longer I could hold on before I had to fuck her.

I willed my body to relax and enjoy the moment, but the second her soapy hands reached down to stroke my cock in rhythm with her breasts sliding across my chest, I knew I'd reached the end of my endurance.

I thought about taking her from behind, like I had the night before, but I wasn't willing to lose the exquisite sensation of her slippery breasts moving against me.

Fortunately, I'd had a bench built into the enormous shower for just this kind of situation.

Backing up, I drew Leigha with me, never losing contact with her.

Moving by feel, I sat down, sliding my hands to her ass, and pulled her to straddle my lap.

There was plenty of room for her knees to slide in beside my hips as I fit my cock to her pussy. She was wet for me and still so tight. Her eyes half closed, she trembled above me, waiting.

This was what I was coming to love about her, this combination of submission and strength.

She wasn't a pushover or weak. So far Leigha was smart, with a strong personality, even if she did need to work on her self-esteem. She didn't seem to understand how beautiful she was, especially hovering over the tip of my cock.

She knew instinctively that I needed control and she gave me that control without question, trusting me to make it good for her, and I would.

I hesitated for just a second, taking in the sight of her rounded body, gleaming from the water, shaking in need.

I wasn't going to last long once I got inside that tight pussy.

"Ride me," I said, clamping my hands on her round ass. She was so much woman, perfectly shaped, soft and curvy wherever I touched, not too much and definitely not too little.

Leigha obeyed, as I'd known she would, pressing her

body into mine until she'd taken every inch of my cock. She looked at me, her eyes locked onto mine. The sight of her nerves draining away, replaced by sheer lust, was too much.

I kissed her, taking her head in my hands, leaving her free to move on me however she liked. She rode me hard, her tits stroking my chest with each thrust of her pussy on my cock.

Tiny moans echoed off the marble walls of the shower until she broke our kiss, breathing hard, crying out my name as she came.

At the sharp sound of her ecstasy, I let go, pulled into my own orgasm by the fierce clenching of her wet heat around my cock.

When we were done, we sat there, pounded by the water, getting our breath back.

I'd been right.

While it wasn't what I'd planned for our encounters, letting Leigha take a little bit of control had paid off. I loved having her on top, putting those lush breasts within easy reach.

I stood, placing her gently on her feet. Before I left her to finish her shower, I kissed her temple, somehow unable to walk away from her.

CHAPTER TWELVE

LEIGHA

As soon as Dylan was gone, I sank back onto the bench. Holy shit. I'd thought the night before had been hot.

Then, he hadn't really let me do much other than follow his lead. I don't really know where I got the idea to wash him, but the sight of him fully naked, in the bright light of the bathroom, was too much.

If that body was the result, I fully approved of him getting up early to hit the gym. I'd known he was tall, with broad shoulders and a narrow waist, based on the way he wore his suits.

Seeing Dylan fully naked was a completely different story. Defined pecs, six pack abs and a tight butt, with well-muscled legs. Even his feet were sexy.

I saw the soap, and it seemed like the perfect excuse to get my hands all over him.

I don't know where I got the idea to clean him with my breasts. I'd never done anything like that before, but by the time I'd washed half his body, I was so crazy with lust it felt like a perfectly normal idea.

I had to do that again. The scrape of his chest hair against my nipples, the heated flare in his eyes every time I wiggled and slid my breasts against him - it was the hottest thing I'd ever done, aside from actually having sex with him.

The sex had been different this time. It's not that I had any complaints about the night before. He'd come three times, once in my mouth and twice while we were having sex.

I'd come four times.

Four times! It had been amazing, hot and passionate. This was more. His mouth on mine, our eyes connecting as I moved on top of him, that gentle kiss to my temple as he left the shower. This time, it felt like more than sex.

Shaking my head at myself, I rinsed one more time under the rainfall showerhead and turned the water off. No spinning daydreams out of Dylan Kane, I told myself. You made a deal.

He wants to fuck you for the weekend, not make you his girlfriend or fall in love with you. Do not get attached. Take the orgasms, rub your sisters' noses in your unbelievably hot date, and then let it go.

I was trying to listen to myself. The last thing I needed was another broken heart after what happened with Steven.

Not that he really broke my heart, but the humiliation and anger over what he'd done was bad enough. I didn't need to fall for a billionaire playboy who was only looking for a good time.

Resolving to stay in control of my emotions, I concentrated on putting on my lotion, drying my hair and adding some makeup so I looked a little more sophisticated.

I needed all the armor I could get if I was going to keep up with Dylan.

I emerged from the bathroom wrapped in a towel, to find my clothes hadn't been put away neatly like my toiletries.

I checked the walk-in closet and found mainly Dylan's things, rows of suits, dress shoes, casual wear, all neatly folded or hung in a closet bigger than my bedroom at home.

In a small section near the door, I discovered a few items of women's clothing. Three dresses, two pairs of jeans I knew cost several hundred dollars each. A few blouses, two tailored skirts and a selection of shoes. Beside it all, a drawer full of lingerie.

All of it top quality. I was pretty sure I recognized the black spike heels with the distinctive red sole as Louboutins.

Exactly the kind of clothes a woman who belonged with Dylan Kane would wear.

My heart sank. There was no commitment between us, but I wasn't a cheater. I didn't cheat on my own boyfriend and not with someone else's.

He'd been so open with me in front of his employees, I'd assumed that meant he didn't have anything to hide.

Maybe he didn't.

He was obscenely wealthy, he owned the casino, and he was well known. If I read the paper more often, I would have recognized him on sight at the bar.

Maybe his girlfriend didn't care if he had fun on the side as long as she got to hang part of her exclusive designer wardrobe in his penthouse closet.

I sat on the bench in the middle of the closet, my stomach twisting in disappointment, trying to figure out what to do.

I wanted to stay.

Dylan was charming. He was fun, and he was the best sex I'd ever had by far. I only had until Sunday with him anyway, which was barely two days.

I wasn't the one with a girlfriend. I was unattached. I could do whatever I wanted.

No you can't. Sleeping with someone else's boyfriend will make you feel like shit. You know it will. And it would. I already felt guilty and, while I *had* slept with another woman's boyfriend, at least I'd done it unknowingly.

If I didn't leave, I'd be doing it on purpose. The whole idea made me feel cheap.

Sure, making a deal to sleep with a guy in exchange for his pretending to be my boyfriend for the weekend wasn't exactly classy, but when I'd thought we were both free it had seemed like fun.

Crazy, unexpected, not like me at all kind of fun. Now it didn't feel like fun at all.

I stood, cinched my towel tighter around my chest, and prepared to face Dylan.

I would rather have done it in anything other than a towel, but I still didn't know where my clothes were and I wasn't going to borrow his girlfriend's, not that they would fit. Any girlfriend of Dylan's serious enough to have her clothes in his closet would be skinny and perfect

Dylan was standing in the living room of the penthouse, dressed in faded jeans and an unbuttoned white shirt, his sexy feet bare on the polished wood floor.

He had his phone to his ear, talking in a low voice as he absently took in the view through the window. Seeing me, he said a quick goodbye and hung up.

I looked around the room, avoiding Dylan's eyes, feeling my cheeks heat at the sight of the tall window behind him.

I'd let him fuck me against that window. Let him show

me to the room service waiter. I hadn't felt ashamed then. I did now.

"Do you want me to order breakfast in, or would you rather go out?" he asked, still holding the phone in his hand.

"I, uh, I can't have breakfast. I have to go," I stuttered out, backing away from his suddenly narrowed eyes.

"Where do you have to go?" he asked, in a smooth, calm voice that didn't match his eyes. "Did something happen?"

"No. I just...have to go."

I backed away as he rounded the coffee table. In my head I was berating him for making me a cheater, for betraying a woman who'd put her trust in him, for being just another asshole.

The angry words rattled in my brain, unable to reach my mouth. They felt too vulnerable, as if I'd let him hurt me when we didn't have that kind of relationship.

He'd never promised me anything other than a date for the weekend, and so far he was delivering on that.

I didn't have to stay and be party to his cheating, but I wasn't sure I had a right to my anger or my growing sense of hurt. That was for the girlfriend he'd betrayed.

I didn't want him to know he'd gotten to me. I might have unwisely developed some feelings for him, but I was going to keep them to myself.

"Tell me why you have to go, Leigha," he said, stalking closer.

"I...I can't stay." I took another few steps backwards, toward the door.

"Are you alright?" He'd reached me by then, taking my arms in his hands, halting my backward progress.

"I'm fine. I just want to go home."

"Why? And don't tell me you're fine. You look miserable. Tell me what's wrong."

"I was looking for my clothes," I said, yet again unable to refuse a direct order from this man.

"And?"

"And I found her things. Your girlfriend's clothes."

"I don't think so," he said, the side of his mouth curling up. The sight of his amusement was too much. I tore myself away, stepping back until my shoulders hit the door of the penthouse.

"I did. I'm not a cheater. I'm not going to stay here with you like this while there's another woman out there thinking you're hers. I can't. The deal is off. Thank you for last night and everything, but I'm going." On the tail of my little speech, I whirled to open the door.

"You're leaving like that? Practically naked? No purse?" Now he sounded like he was laughing at me. I fumed, frustration and disappointment welling in my chest until I felt my eyes fill.

"Where are my things?" I demanded. He reached for me, but I slapped his hand away. "Tell me where my things are so I can leave."

"What if I told you my girlfriend wouldn't care that you were here?" He asked, reaching for me again. I ducked away, retreating into the living room where I could get some space from him.

"I care," I said, humiliated by the tears coursing down my cheeks. Why wouldn't he just give me my things and let me go?

"Please just give me my clothes and my purse so I can leave."

I remembered bringing my purse up with me, but it was nowhere to be seen now. It was going to be bad enough to go to the rehearsal dinner and wedding dateless after showing up with Dylan last night.

I couldn't imagine how awful it would be if I had to call my Mom from the lobby, wearing nothing but a towel, and ask her to let me in her room. Too late, I wished I'd asked her for her room number the night before, but there hadn't been a reason to think I'd need it.

"Give me my things, Dylan. Please," I asked again, wishing I could have done this without crying. I wanted to be strong and fierce. Righteous. Not defeated.

"No," Dylan said. He was across the room before I could think up an escape route. He grabbed for my arms again, this time catching hold before I could push him away.

He held me still with one hand while the other snatched the end of my loosening towel and tugged it free. Fresh tears spilled from my eyes.

As if this hadn't been humiliating enough, now I was completely naked. Dylan pulled me close, plastering me to the length of his body, his arms a steel cage around me.

His heat was a discordant comfort, the last thing I wanted touching me and yet somehow soothing.

I yanked back against him, to no effect. I was trapped.

"You're not leaving me," he said, bending his head until his lips reached my ear. "Not until I decide you can go. And I'm not done with you yet."

"You are. I'm not staying here with you. I didn't want it to be this way. I thought you'd tell me if there was someone else before we started this."

I hated the hitch in my voice. I'd never been an easy crier, but frustration always got me. The added hurt and disappointment of realizing Dylan was a cheating asshole didn't help.

"I would have," he said. "There isn't someone else."

"Don't lie to me," I whispered into his chest. I was losing my fight. It was over, so why couldn't he just let me leave? He couldn't think that after all this, I was going to give in and stay.

"I'm not lying."

Before I could stop him, he scooped me up in his arms and carried me to his bedroom, holding me as if I didn't weigh anything.

I hadn't been carried by anyone since I was a child, and the novel sensation was so shocking it slowed my reaction.

He had me in his room before I began to push at his shoulders. His grip was rock solid. I wasn't getting down until he put me down.

When we reached the small section of women's clothes in his closet, he returned me to my feet. Hands on my shoulders, ready to stop me if I offered further resistance, he said,

"Look at them."

"What do you mean?" I didn't understand. I was looking at them. They were beautiful clothes, so who wouldn't look? He let out a low growl of annoyance.

"Don't move," he said, and reached for a navy blue sundress splashed with brightly colored flowers. Pulling it off the hanger, he folded back the bodice and tore out the price tag before unzipping the dress and dropping it over my head.

I couldn't quite catch up. My eyes focused on a little black dress beside the empty hanger.

I saw a flash of white and realized it, too, still had its tag. So did the jeans. I'd missed that before. Embarrassment and hope tangled inside me as I let Dylan lead me into the bathroom.

He zipped the back of the sundress, drawing the fabric snug around my torso.

I never would have picked a dress like this for myself. I

would have thought the straps too thin and the top too skimpy for my breasts. I would have been wrong.

The sundress highlighted my curves without overexposing them, making the most of my breasts while my waist looked small in comparison. I met Dylan's eyes in the mirror, unable to think of a single thing to say.

"Those are your clothes, Leigha."

"What? Why? Where are my things?" When did he have time to buy me clothes?

"Your things are still packed in your suitcases," he said, stroking my hair off my shoulders as we both took in the perfect fit of the dress.

"Can I have them back?" I asked. I liked this dress better than anything I'd packed, but I still needed my things. My wardrobe wasn't big enough that I could sacrifice a whole suitcase of it.

"No," Dylan answered. "I don't think I trust you with it. If you'd had it, you would have snuck out on me, wouldn't you?"

"I don't know," I said, "Maybe."

"Why didn't you just ask me?" He actually looked confused.

For a man who seemed to have all the moves when it came to women, it was clear there were some things he really didn't get.

Maybe I should have felt bad about my false accusation, but I was pretty sure any other woman would have had the same reaction to finding another woman's clothes in the closet of the man they were sleeping with.

I just shook my head in response. If he didn't get why I'd been a little irrational, I wasn't going to be able to explain it to him. Instead, I said, "I really don't like cheating. The idea that you might have a girlfriend made me a little crazy."

He wrapped his arms around me and squeezed. I kept thinking I wasn't the right kind of woman for him, but the sight of us in the bathroom mirror, me cradled in his arms, his face pressed to the top of my head - we looked like we belonged. Placing a soft kiss to the side of my mouth, he said,

"My father cheated on my mom so often he destroyed her. By the time she died when I was fifteen, she was broken inside. She loved him, and he just didn't seem to care. I'm not an angel, but I don't cheat, Leigha. I wouldn't do that to a woman."

I nodded in response, not sure what to say. He kept surprising me. I followed him when he took my hand and walked me back into the bedroom.

"So when did you have time to get all of this?" I gestured to the clothes hanging in the closet.

"Pick a pair of shoes and let's go out. I'll tell you at breakfast."

At the second mention of breakfast, I realized I was starving. I was also ready to ditch all these heavy emotions and go have some fun.

After I put on some underwear. The top drawer beside the hanging clothes was filled with lingerie. Lace and silk panties, negligees, bras, and other bits of fluff overflowed the drawer.

The dress had built in support, so I didn't need a bra, but there was no way I was leaving the penthouse without panties. I wasn't that bold. I slipped on a pair of lacy bikinis and pulled them up, taking my time when I felt Dylan's eyes on my exposed legs and butt.

Now for some shoes. Beside the Louboutins, I spotted a pair of navy platform sandals with a flat bow at the toe and sexy ribbon straps around the ankle.

They were sweet, sassy, and perfect for the dress. As I reached for them, I spotted the imprint inside the shoe. Kate Spade. Not quite as unattainable as the Louboutins, but still way above my normal shoe budget, unless I decided not to eat for a month.

I slipped them on, fastening the buckles hidden beneath the ribbons. They were so cute. I was in love with these shoes. With the whole outfit, actually.

I suspected I'd love the rest of what he'd bought me just as much. Resolving to push away my concerns and have some fun, I let Dylan take my hand and lead me from the room.

CHAPTER THIRTEEN

LEIGHA

Dylan brought me to Veranda at the Four Seasons, where we ate outside by the pool at a secluded table for two. Once we were seated, he explained,

"We'll have more privacy here than at the Delecta. And I wanted to see you in that dress out in the sunshine."

"I've always wanted to eat here," I said, taking in the elegant surroundings, quiet on a Friday morning.

"Why haven't you?"

"I keep meaning to, but I get busy with work and things that have to get done and I don't end up getting out much."

It was sadly true. I'd taken the job in Vegas after college mostly because Haywood and Cross was a great company. Partly, too, because I'd thought being in Vegas might give me an opportunity to have some fun.

Instead, I ended up living the same life I'd always lived if you substituted going to work for studying and classes. There was so much to explore in this city and I was an expert on my neighborhood yoga studio and grocery store.

When this weekend was over, I wasn't going to crawl back into my shell. I was going to try to experience life a little more, even if it wasn't on the same level as hanging out with a sexy billionaire.

Picking up the menu, I tried to figure out what to get. I wanted something decadent, but I thought I should order the fruit plate, or the Quinoa Muesli Cereal. That felt like a waste in a place like this.

Dylan took over, asking, "Do you mind if I order for you? Is there anything you won't eat?"

"No, you can order." I put the menu down, relieved. Dylan seemed to like me as I was, but I still felt weird about ordering a fattening breakfast in front of him. It was stupid. I knew that.

I was an adult woman and I should be able to eat waffles or a Danish if I wanted one. I'm not sure if the leftovers of childhood ever go away. Too many years of my sisters critiquing every bite I put in my mouth still left me weird about eating in public. I needed to get over it.

The waiter returned and my mouth watered as Dylan ordered the Limón ricotta pancakes for himself and the tiramisu French toast for me. It was exactly what I would have ordered for myself if I'd had the courage.

When the waiter left, I picked up my coffee and said, "So, the clothes? Did you go shopping in the middle of the night? Or do you keep special fairies on staff who do your bidding at all hours?"

"The second, in a way. Not a fairy, my assistant, Melissa."

"The one I met at your office last night? I thought her name was Cheryl."

"It is. Cheryl handles my office. Melissa takes care of personal things."

"Personal things? Like what? Does she pick your dates up for you?" I was half-kidding and half sure he was going to say 'Yes'.

"Not usually. Though she has made an airport pick-up or two for me."

"You fly your dates in? Like a lingerie model with a shoot in Bali coming to Vegas just so you can take her out to dinner?"

This time I really was kidding. I swallowed my amusement when Dylan took a slow sip of coffee, his eyes steady on my face, but said nothing.

Of course he flew in models to date. Women around the globe were probably begging for the chance to go out with him.

Again, I wondered what he was doing with me. Finally, he said, "I don't want to talk about any other women right now."

"Fair enough," I said. I didn't want to talk about his other women either, especially after my embarrassing fit earlier. "So what else does Melissa do?"

"She coordinates my life. The past twenty-four hours aside, I spend most of my time working. I don't have time to go shopping, make dentist appointments, or get my car serviced. I have to throw a number of parties and other social events that are mostly work and I don't have the time, or the inclination, to handle those either. Melissa takes care of everything I can't. Or don't want to."

"Okay, that actually makes sense. So when did she go buy all this? We only met last night. How did she know what to get?"

"I texted her to take a look at what you had, and if she thought I'd agree, she should open the boutiques downstairs and get you set up."

"So she didn't like my clothes?" I asked, not sure how to feel about a stranger going through my things and deciding they needed to be replaced. I wasn't a fashionista, but I thought I did alright on my junior accountant's salary. Dylan shrugged.

"Maybe. But Melissa likes clothes. She may have thought yours were fine, but taken the excuse to buy you new things anyway." That made me feel somewhat better. If I had the budget to buy clothes like this, I'd jump on it, even if they weren't for me.

"So you made her work late? What if she had other plans?" I knew I was being nosy, but the whole concept of him having a person who would jump to do anything he asked was fascinating to me.

"I pay Melissa extremely well to never have other plans when I need her for something. She's on call twenty-four-seven and she makes enough money that she doesn't mind her hours. Plus, she likes me." He gave me a satisfied grin, teasing me.

"Yeah, I bet she does," I said, smiling back.

"She's happily married to a lawyer who works long hours, no kids, which is part of why she doesn't mind me calling her in at odd times. She's one of those people who needs to be busy."

"Hmm," I said, unable to relate.

I suspected Dylan was like that, always on the go. Anyone who ran a business empire had to be. That was not me.

I worked hard at my job, but in my off time, I was more than happy to lie around, reading a book and snacking on chocolate. Probably part of the reason I still hadn't seen that much of Vegas.

The waiter returned with our plates, sliding in front of

me a beautifully presented stack of the tiramisu French toast with a banana-apple compote and citrus mascarpone cream. Heaven.

The scents coming off my plate were so delicious I wanted to cry with joy. Chocolate, espresso, cream, and powdered sugar scented the air. If it tasted as good as it looked and smelled, I was going to be a very happy woman.

Dylan's Limón ricotta pancakes with fig compote looked equally tempting. Reading my mind, and eyeing my French toast, he said, "I thought we could share."

"Works for me." He cut a bite of pancake with his fork and brought it to my mouth. The taste of sweet lemon burst across my tongue. Withdrawing the fork from between my lips, he scooped up a bite of my French toast for himself.

"This place is always excellent," he said. We ate like that for the next few minutes. I fed him a bite, he did the same for me. The intimacy was new.

I'd eaten breakfast with men before, but this felt like we were in our own little island, just Dylan and me, with nothing to worry about but enjoying our meal and each other.

Our plates were empty before I knew it. Dylan sat back with his coffee, studying me. I tucked a stray lock of hair behind my ear, self-conscious again. Picking up my own coffee, I said, "What?"

"Just glad you ate all your breakfast. You're going to need your energy today."

"Why? What are we doing?" I hoped we were going straight back to his penthouse where he could strip this dress off and fuck me for the rest of the day. Not that I was greedy or anything, but I only had him until Sunday. I wanted as much of Dylan as I could get.

"We're going shopping," he said, drinking half of his

coffee before setting the cup back in its saucer. He checked his watch and gestured to the waiter. "The shops should be opening by the time we get there."

"Why are we going shopping?" I asked. Hadn't he already bought me more than I could possibly wear this weekend?

"Because I want to take you shopping," he said, as if that was the end of the conversation.

Maybe to him, it was. I wasn't exactly comfortable with the idea of Dylan taking me shopping. We'd made a deal - he would be my date, and I'd sleep with him for the weekend. At the time, it had felt like an even trade.

Five orgasms later, I was pretty sure I was getting the best part of the exchange. Fantastic, mind-blowing sex with a ridiculously hot guy, and a date for the wedding from hell.

Not to mention the money he'd already spent on the clothes he'd asked his assistant to buy. They weren't flashy, but I knew the designers well enough to know that there was at least several thousand dollars hanging in the closet upstairs, not to mention the dress, panties and sandals I was wearing at the moment.

Part of me was dying to see what his idea of going shopping was, but it felt weird. It was too much for a weekend fling.

"I don't need anything else. You've already bought me too much. We can go back to the room instead," I said, hopefully. His smile sent a jolt of arousal straight between my legs.

"We'll go back to the room. Later. First, I want to go shopping."

"Why? Really, it's not necessary."

At that, he laughed. "Of course it's not necessary. Does it have to be necessary? Or does it offend your accountant's heart to spend money on something you don't strictly need?"

I looked away, too embarrassed to admit he'd figured me out. He laughed again. "Get over it. We're going shopping. Please tell me you aren't in the wedding."

I shook my head. "No. Thank God. Cathie is the maid of honor and Christie has her friends as bridesmaids."

"Then we're at least getting you a new dress for the wedding. And making a stop at La Perla. Or Agent Provocatuer. Maybe both. And more shoes, I think."

I was completely speechless. I bought my underwear from a catalogue. It was nice enough, I thought. He hadn't seemed to mind when he'd stripped it off of me. But I'd never owned anything like La Perla or Agent Provocatuer.

Dylan was right, the idea of spending hundreds of dollars for a bra, or a pair of panties, was beyond my bank account or my sensibilities. Besides, I was more than happy to skip clothes of all kinds for the rest of the weekend. Except for the rehearsal dinner and the wedding itself.

Dylan, in what I was learning was his typical style, ran right over my objections. He hooked his arm through mine and we walked through the hotel to valet parking, where his Maserati was waiting.

A short drive later, we passed the car off to yet another valet attendant and entered the first floor of Neiman Marcus. I'd browsed here before, but I'd rarely shopped.

I tried to slow Dylan's pace so I could take in the displays, but he steered me straight to the escalators. Apparently, he knew where he was going.

CHAPTER FOURTEEN

LEIGHA

The next thing I knew I was standing in the women's department surrounded by lovely cocktail dresses, listening to Dylan say,

"Tell Lola that Dylan Kane is here. She's expecting me."

The clerk nodded her head and said, "Yes, sir," before she disappeared into the back of the store.

"Lola is my personal shopper. She'll take good care of us." He smiled down at me with something that looked like affection.

My knees went weak. Still feeling a little vulnerable from my freak-out that morning, I reminded myself to be on my guard with him. We were just having fun. It didn't mean anything.

"So Melissa doesn't buy your clothes, too?" I teased. Dylan smiled, and the crinkle around his green eyes when he did made me wish we were alone.

"No. She doesn't have the time. And Lola knows every

square inch of Neiman's. She could assemble a complete wardrobe in twenty minutes if she had to."

"Dylan, you flatter me."

I turned to see a mature woman walking toward us, her honey colored hair twisted into a loose bun, her smile friendly.

Reaching out, she took Dylan's offered hand, then leaned in to kiss his cheek. I couldn't quite place her faint accent. Not Spanish, but close. She released Dylan's hand and turned to face me.

"What have you brought me this morning?" Her eyebrows lifted, her expression expectant.

"Lola, this is my friend Leigha Carmichael. Leigha, Lola."

I extended my hand, not sure how to read her. She wasn't flirting with Dylan, which was a surprise and a relief. They seemed to share an easy, friendly camaraderie.

It made me a little shy, though. If she was friendly with him, how would she feel about him buying clothes for some woman he barely knew? Would she think I was a gold digger? Before I could stress out too much about it, I found my hand clasped between both of hers.

"Lovely, just lovely," she said to Dylan.

To me, she leaned closer, as if telling a secret, and said, "You know, Dylan has never brought me a woman to dress. I've sent him some bits and pieces over the years, but has he ever introduced me to a young lady? No."

She shook her head, her flair for drama making me smile. "We're going to have some fun today."

"Oh, no, I think you misunderstood," I started to say. Dylan's hand over my mouth cut me off.

"Leigha needs a dress to wear to an evening wedding. Something appropriate, but I want it to be the best dress in the room. And we'd like to see anything else you have that might look good on her. Anything."

From the emphasis he put on the last word, I was pretty sure he was asking her to pick out lingerie. I blushed at the thought. Dylan caught my pink cheeks and smiled.

"Lola is right," he whispered in my ear. "We're going to have fun."

And we did, at least for a while. Lola ushered us to the back of the store, through a set of double doors and into a private lounge.

After leaving us with a bottle of champagne and asking me a few questions about sizes and preferred styles, she vanished. She returned ten minutes and one glass of champagne later followed by an assistant who struggled to keep up.

Hanging several dresses on a nearby rack, she murmured instructions to the assistant and sent her back into the store. To me, she said,

"Alright, miss. Up and into the dressing room please. I have a few selections for us to try."

Putting down my glass, I followed her into the small room. On the wall, she hung two dresses. One was a color block dress with ivory scalloped lace on top, and black satin from the ribcage down to the high-low hem finished in eyelets.

The other was its opposite, a confection of strapless black tulle and satin, embroidered all over with delicate silver daisies. Neither was a dress I would have chosen for myself, and not just because I was sure they cost more than my car was worth. As if she didn't notice my hesitation, Lola said,

"The de la Renta first, please." At my blank look, she smiled and gently explained, "The black and ivory, dear."

She slipped out of the dressing room, giving me privacy to strip off the navy flowered sundress and contemplate the designer dress hanging in front of me.

To my surprise, it slipped on easily, fitting itself to my curves as if it had been made for me. I did up as much of the zipper as I could and gaped at my reflection in the mirror. The dress was aggressively sexy.

On another woman, one with a straighter, smaller body, it might simply be elegant. On me, it revealed the full curves of my breasts, made my waist look tiny and the hi-low hemline showed off the best part of my legs.

I looked modern, edgy, and sexual. I was afraid to look at the price tag. A soft knock on the door startled me.

"Yes?"

"Do you need help with the zipper?" Lola asked.

"Please."

She slipped in and circled around me, examining the fit of the dress. Without comment, she stopped behind me and pulled the zipper the rest of the way up.

Her hands twisted in my hair, doing something that ended up with the thick mass of it piled on my head in a makeshift up-do, secured by a glittery clip she'd snapped into place.

Dropping to her knees, Lola eased my bare feet into equally glittery gold heels. A moment later, I looked ready to stroll into a gala. Speechless, I stared at myself in the mirror. Lola stood beside me, grinning.

"I am amazing, am I not?"

I grinned back at her. She was gone ten minutes, and she came back with this?

"Amazing doesn't cover it," I said, squeezing her hand in a thank you. Even if I never wore it, getting to play dress up in Oscar de la Renta was the most fun I'd had in ages. Outside of having sex with Dylan.

"Let's see what Dylan thinks," she said. I followed her out of the dressing room, eager to see Dylan's reaction. He didn't disappoint.

As I stepped out of the dressing room, he rose, following Lola and me to the three-way mirror. Much as Lola had, he circled me, examining me. Unlike Lola, his eyes were possessive. Predatory. Standing behind me, he met my eyes in the mirror.

"Do you like it?" he asked.

"Do you?" I thought it looked fantastic, but I wasn't confident enough to say so out loud.

"You look gorgeous. Sexy. Powerful. I won't be able to leave your side or the men will be all over you. But we won't get it unless you like it."

"I like it," I said in a whisper, my head spinning from Dylan's words. I thought I looked good, but the way he described me melted my heart.

"Then we'll get it. And the shoes. Go try on the other one." He kissed the side of my mouth.

"But-" If we were getting this one, I didn't need another dress.

"Humor me," he said. "If Lola brought two dresses, you should try on the other one."

"Okay." Lola trailed me to the dressing room. After helping me with the zipper, she discretely slipped out, saying,

"If you need help with the bustier, let me know."

I glanced down at the bench beside the hanging dresses to see a black satin bustier. Looking at the other dress, I realized it was strapless. I'd need something more beneath to hold me, and the dress, in place.

Carefully removing the ivory and black de la Renta I was wearing, I replaced it on its hanger before turning to the bustier.

Getting it on was a little bit of a battle, but I wasn't ready for the svelte Lola to see me mostly naked.

She'd been nothing but kind, and I had no reason to think she'd sneer at me. Still, I was too shy to ask for help with my underwear. In the end, I fastened most of the hook and eyes in the front, then wiggled it around and settled it in place. Lola could do the last few once I had the dress on.

And what a dress. If the black and white de la Renta was elegant and sexy, this was a grown woman's fairytale.

An underdress of black satin provided the framework for yards and yards of transparent, shimmering black tulle embroidered with delicate silver daisies. I lowered the zipper, peeking at the label inside the bodice. Carolina Herrera.

Wow. I loved her dresses, but had never dreamed of even trying one on, much less owning one. Unable to resist, I looked for the price tag. Somehow, I wasn't surprised to find it was missing. That was probably for the best.

I didn't really want to know what it cost. I could guess, and the guess was enough to freak me out if I thought about it too much.

Stepping into the gown, I pushed the cost out of my mind. I'd made it clear to Dylan that he didn't have to buy me anything. He'd made it equally clear that he wanted to. Who was I to argue?

I eased the dress up, tugging it gently over the curve of my breasts. When I had the zipper mostly up, I called softly to Lola. A moment later, the door opened, and she stepped inside. Fastening the last hooks of the bustier and the rest of the zipper, she smoothed the fabric over my hips and sighed.

"You look like a princess. All you're missing are your slippers."

Avoiding my reflection in the mirror, I took the sparkling sandals from her and slipped them on, admiring the crystal embellished straps and delicate bows setting off the silver spike heels.

If Cinderella had a choice other than glass, she would have gone for these shoes. Apt, since I was turning back into a pumpkin in two days. Everything buckled, zipped and hooked into place, I risked a glance in the mirror.

"Oh, wow," I breathed at my reflection. I looked like a princess. Both dresses were too formal for Christie's wedding, and I'd never have a chance to wear either one again. But my heart squeezed in my chest as I saw myself in the dressing room mirror.

I didn't look drab, plump, or boring. My skin glowed against the shimmering black tulle, my grey eyes seemed lit from within, my full breasts curving beautifully but contained in the bodice of the dress, my waist nipped in, looking smaller than I knew it was.

I met Lola's eyes as I turned to open the door. Her smile told me I looked as good in the dress as I thought I did. Stepping out of the dressing room, I waited to see what Dylan would say.

CHAPTER FIFTEEN

DYLAN

I'd been checking my messages on my phone when I heard the handle turn on the dressing room door. Looking up, I got my first glimpse of Leigha in the second dress. I froze, my usually razor sharp brain on lock down.

She stood there, in fairytale crystal heels and a fantasy of a dress, her eyes as open and vulnerable as I'd ever seen them. I knew, somewhere in the back of my mind, that I needed to say something. She was insecure about her looks.

That was easy enough to figure out, and a little nervous about letting me buy her expensive clothes. Most women would be trying to see how much they could get out of me, but not Leigha.

She stood completely still, waiting for my reaction. I didn't know what to say. Every word in my vocabulary was inadequate to describe the picture she made.

Beautiful would be true, but not enough. She was grace and elegance, lovely and sexy at the same time. The luscious curves of her tits and ass combined with her clear, intelligent, grey eyes and her smooth, creamy skin, all wrapped in that amazing dress. She was mine.

She had to be. I couldn't let something this precious get away from me.

Lola's low murmur brought me back to my senses, and I noticed Leigha's open expression beginning to falter. She thought I didn't like it. Clearing my throat, I said,

"We'll take both of them. And we'd like to see a selection of daytime and cocktail dresses. Lingerie as well."

"Yes, sir."

Lola and her assistant disappeared, leaving me alone with Leigha. It had only been a few hours since I'd fucked her in the shower. It felt like an eternity.

If she was a different women, I'd already be backing her into the dressing room, stripping off that $10,000 dress and fucking her from behind against the full length mirror.

I'd let her keep on the fairytale shoes. It would be like fucking an angel. Having been in that pussy, I knew it would feel like fucking Heaven.

Sadly, Leigha was not that woman. Pushing her boundaries was one thing. I planned to do a lot of that. But in her heart, Leigha was a good girl.

Trying to fuck her in what was essentially Lola's office would not go over well. I resigned myself to waiting until we got back to the hotel.

My original plan had been to take her to one of the high-end lingerie stores and play with her in the privacy of their dressing rooms.

Not anymore. I didn't want to wait. Lola's selection was good enough. We could save the trip to Agent Provocateur for another day.

"Dylan?" I heard Leigha whisper. Turning to face her, I reached out for her hand. "Is it okay?" she asked.

I still had no idea what to say. Taking the easy way out, I closed the distance between us and took her face in my hands.

Her lips were soft under mine, yielding sweetly to me as I kissed away her doubt. Not trusting myself, I kept my touch isolated to her face, holding her still as our kiss went wild.

I'd meant to reassure her, but once I had her taste it wasn't enough. Her mouth, the tiny whimpers in her throat as my tongue tangled with hers, it all drove me to the edge.

I couldn't remember the last time a kiss was enough to get me this hard, this fast. I kept her there, teetering on her heels, her mouth feeding from mine, until the scuff of Lola's shoe betrayed that we were no longer alone. I broke away and whispered in her ear,

"You're more beautiful than I imagined a woman could be. Try this stuff on fast so we can get back to the Delecta and I can fuck you until you can't walk."

After a moment of silence, Leigha fell into me, her body shaking with giggles. She gasped for breath, her shoulders trembling, tits jiggling in the strapless bodice in a way that did not help my cock go soft. When she finally had herself under control, she whispered back,

"That is both the most romantic and the crudest thing anyone has ever said to me."

"If that was the crudest thing anyone has ever said to you, we're going to have to expand your horizons."

CHAPTER SIXTEEN

LEIGHA

The glint in his eye when he talked about expanding my horizons made my knees weak. Before I could think of what to say, Lola was ushering me back into the dressing room.

The next hour was a whirlwind of rattling hangers, zippers, and quick trips into the lounge to show Dylan what I was wearing.

Cocktail dresses, their fabric fine, colors dark and dramatic, each dress with shoes to match. Day dresses, not unlike the one I'd worn earlier in the day. My head spun.

I lost my nerves about Lola seeing me in my underwear, giving in to her relentless urgings to try this and that. Dylan wanted us to move quickly, and it seemed Dylan got what he wanted.

I lost track of how many things I'd tried on or what Dylan liked. I never even saw most of the underwear. Lola had me try on one bra, made of the thinnest pale pink silk, before whisking it off and calling "thirty-six D" to her assistant.

I caught sight of the letters 'erla' on the bra and knew it had to be La Perla. I swallowed hard. I had no idea what the dresses I'd tried on since the ball gown cost, but I knew about La Perla.

I'd drooled over La Perla.

Dylan was crazy to be spending this kind of money on a woman he'd never see again after this weekend.

I, on the other hand, was not crazy. Exchanging my body for a wedding date notwithstanding, I wasn't a fool. He was a billionaire, and he wanted to shower me with a ridiculously expensive wardrobe. I wasn't going to say no.

When I left him, I'd be walking away from the best sex of my life--amazing, life changing sex with a man who managed to be both domineering and sweet. Just the thought of him touching me got me wet.

I knew dating other men after this would be even more of a letdown than dating had been before Dylan. That hadn't exactly been anything special. At least I'd have an unbelievable wardrobe to console me.

Maybe there was a bright side to leaving Dylan so quickly. Eventually he'd show that he was an asshole. In my experience, most men did if I gave them enough time.

A hot, brilliant, billionaire? It was too much to hope that he was as sweet and caring as he seemed. No, anything that seemed too good to be true always was. At least this way I'd be leaving before I saw the jerk hiding inside his perfect exterior.

We brought only the black and white dress and matching shoes back to the penthouse. Lola had arranged for the rest to be delivered later in the day.

Dylan barely spoke on the ride back to the Delecta, his jaw tight, eyes on the road. I might have worried about his closed expression, but his hand on my leg, fingertips tracing circles on the sensitive skin of my inner thigh, convinced me that he was just focused on getting home as fast as he could.

He held himself in check until we were behind the heavy doors of the penthouse. The second they shut, he tossed the dress to the floor and swung me around until my back hit the door.

A breath later, his hands were under my dress, tearing off my panties. He lifted me, fingers gripping my ass as my legs wrapped around his waist.

My head dropped back, thudding into the door as he filled me, the stretch of his cock more than welcome after wanting him all day.

It went fast, his face dropped into my neck, his breath against my skin, the pressure between my legs building with every thrust. I heard myself crying out his name as I came, the sound sobbing out as the pleasure overwhelmed me.

I think Dylan came with me, but I wasn't sure since he never really went soft.

Still inside me, he carried me back to the bed and lowered us down, pulling off my dress as we went.

Needing to feel his skin on mine, I tore at his shirt until my breasts pressed to his warm chest. I reached for his face, wanting the connection of his mouth on mine.

He gave me what I wanted, kissing me with hunger as he started fucking me again. I wouldn't have thought I could come again so quickly. I would have been wrong.

Later, after drifting into sleep draped over Dylan, his hand possessively clamped on my ass, I woke to find myself alone in the bed.

After a quick visit to the bathroom, I pulled on the button down shirt I'd torn off Dylan earlier and went looking for him.

As he had that morning, he stood at the window, phone

to his ear, this time bare-chested. Yum. When he wasn't spending time with me, it seemed he was working. Catching sight of me in his shirt, his eyes heated.

He gestured to the room service cart in the center of the room. I wasn't sure what time it was, but it felt like breakfast was days ago instead of hours.

Lifting the lids on the trays, I saw a cheeseburger with waffle fries, a grilled salmon sandwich and fish tacos, all still steaming. They must have just been delivered. My stomach growled.

Dylan's arms closed around me. "Hungry?" he asked, kissing the side of my mouth.

"Very," I said, leaning into him. "Sorry I fell asleep on you."

"Don't be. It's my mission to wear you out." I felt the heat hit my cheeks. He'd definitely done that. I was hoping that after we fueled up he'd be willing to do it again. "Which do you want?" He gestured to the food.

"All of it looks good," I said.

"A little of everything?"

"That would be perfect." He began dividing the plates. "Dylan?" I asked, nervous I was going to upset our cozy afternoon. He looked up at me, waiting, eyes narrowed as if he knew he wouldn't like my question.

"I need my purse back. I have to check my phone, see if my Mom called."

"Then you just need your phone," he said.

"Why don't you want to give me my purse?" I asked, confused and a little weirded out.

"I don't trust you yet," he said, bluntly, his eyes meeting mine in a stare that left no room for compromise.

"I'm not going anywhere," I protested.

"This morning, if you'd had your purse, would you have left me?"

I looked away. I would have. I would have run out of here as fast as I could and not looked back. Still, saying he didn't trust me was harsh.

Then again, clearly, I didn't trust him either, or I wouldn't have freaked when I saw the women's clothes in his closet. We'd only known each other a day. Why was trust even an issue?

I could answer that question myself. Because we had a deal, and Dylan thought I was going to bail on my end. After my behavior that morning, I couldn't really argue with his logic, even though keeping my purse was taking it a little far.

"Fine," I said, not wanting to start a fight in the middle of our perfect day. "How about you just let me have my phone?" A long, intent stare. Then he nodded and set the plate he was holding back on the table.

"You eat. I'll get your phone."

He came back a moment later with my phone in his hand. I took it and clicked it on for a quick look. A few texts from a number I didn't recognize, but no calls. I set the phone aside and sat down at my plate, waiting for him to join me.

"So, what do you do?" I asked, curious what had him on the phone all the time.

Sitting across from him and his bare chest, my mind was trolling the gutter. I wanted to make an effort at an actual conversation before we fell on each other again. "I know you run the Delecta and oversee the rest of the company, but what does that mean?"

My job was interesting to me, but fairly routine. I was curious to know what being a billionaire CEO really meant.

In between asking me questions about my own work, I found out that being Dylan meant a ridiculous amount of responsibility, making decisions that affected millions of dollars and thousands of people's jobs every day.

He took his company seriously, seeing it as a family legacy he shared with a brother and cousin, all of whom were based on the east coast. Kane Enterprises had holdings in a wide range of areas, from hospitality, to precious metals, to hospital equipment.

How they stayed on top of everything was beyond my brain's ability to process. I handled my clients' sometimes-complicated financial affairs, and I did it very well. However, what Dylan did was another world of complexity.

When I asked how he managed it all, he said, "I hire the best and I pay them very well. Never underestimate the value of a good team. Without my people, Kane Enterprises wouldn't be what it is."

He was making it hard to keep my heart distant. He could be overbearing and bossy - my missing purse case in point - but when he said things like this, I melted.

So many men in his position would take all the credit. Instead, Dylan deflected it back to his employees. We sat there so long, asking questions and trading stories, I lost track of time.

If my mother hadn't called to ask if I knew where the rehearsal dinner was (I did), I might have forgotten it completely.

Looking at the time, I jumped out of my chair. "I have to start getting ready," I said, eyeing his chest again.

I'd been planning on wearing my hair up that night, since the black and white dress demanded it. But getting my long, thick hair curled and pinned in place would take some time.

If I did what I wanted and got my hands all over him, we'd be late.

Very late.

Dylan glanced at the clock on his phone. "Fine," he said. "First, come here." I did as commanded, mostly because I didn't want to say no to him.

When I was within reach, he yanked me close, wrapping his arms around me. His mouth hit in a rush of heat, his lips opening mine. I sank my hands in his hair, kissing him back, loving the taste of him, the consuming way he kissed me as if he wanted to absorb everything I was.

He was addicting. All too soon, his arms loosened and he let me go. My knees wobbled.

"Go," he said, turning me toward the bedroom. "Get ready for dinner before I call your mother and cancel."

Blindly, I walked away, wondering how mad my Mom would be if we didn't show. Mad. So mad her head would explode. And, as annoying as my sisters could be, I loved my Mom.

An hour later, I was showered, wearing a hotel robe, my hair dried and pinned in sections, ready for the curling iron. As I lifted the iron to wrap the first section of hair, my phone beeped with a text. I put the iron down and reached for my phone.

Don't ignore me, you bitch.

What? I stared at the number, then flipped back through the day's texts. When I'd seen the unfamiliar number earlier, I'd assumed it was a mistake. The texts started at eleven that morning.

Call me.

Where are you? Call me back.

This isn't over. Call me before I come find you.

And then the one from a minute ago: *Don't ignore me, you bitch.*

They had to be a wrong number. No one I knew would send me texts like this, and I'd never seen this phone number before. It was local to Vegas, but so were millions of other numbers.

Only one person had ever talked to me this way, and he was gone. Long gone. Besides, I didn't have anything Steven could want. He'd already cleaned out my savings. I didn't have anything else for him to steal.

Putting the phone back down, I lifted the curling iron and got to work. I only had tonight and tomorrow night with Dylan. I wasn't going to waste them worrying about some stranger's drama that had ended up on my phone.

Doing my hair took almost an hour, but it was worth it. I'd curled each section, then twisted it up and pinned in in a pattern that looked like a mess to start, but ended up an elaborate pinwheel of twists and curls.

I rarely had an excuse to get dressed up, but I'd had long hair my entire life, as well as an addiction to watching styling videos on YouTube. I'd been dying to try this one since I'd seen it months ago. It looked as good as I'd hoped.

Paired with the Oscar de la Renta dress and glittering gold heels, my elaborate hair and evening make-up looked exactly right. Hopefully, Dylan would agree.

I couldn't help feeling a little smug at the thought of what my bitchy sisters would say when they saw me. I wasn't a skinny Minnie, but in this dress it didn't matter. Even my critical eye thought I looked awesome.

On my way out the door, I glanced at my phone, considering. Lola had sent along a selection of evening purses. I needed one for my lip gloss, but I didn't need my phone. Everyone who might call would already be there. As I reached for it, preparing to put it beside the bed, it beeped with another text.

Call me now, you stupid whore.

Another beep. Then,

Don't make me hunt you down, Leigha.

A bolt of ice froze my spine as I sank down to sit on the side of the bed.

Whoever this was, they were after me.

CHAPTER SEVENTEEN

LEIGHA

I stared at the phone on the table as if it were a snake, poised to strike. It remained silent and dark, nothing more than metal, glass, and plastic. Before it could come to life with another creepy message, I turned and left the room.

Whatever was going on, I didn't want to know. Not right now. I wanted to walk out of that room in my fabulous dress, wearing fabulous heels, and go to my evil sister's rehearsal dinner with my unbelievably hot date. That phone, and the powder keg of drama it suddenly represented, was staying behind. Nothing was going to ruin my night with Dylan.

I was so focused on closing the door to the bedroom, I didn't see Dylan until he was standing right in front of me. The guy was knee-weakening hot, normally. Standing before me in a classic black tux, he might have stepped right out of a romantic movie.

More than his good looks, or the way the tux fit his broad shoulders, it was the look on his face that did me in.

Possession, arousal, and admiration swirled in his eyes, telling me that I didn't look as good as I thought I did, I looked better.

Holding out his hand to me, he said, "Come here." I crossed the distance between us, smiling as he drew me into his arms.

"I'm going to ruin your lip gloss," he said, his mouth coming down on mine.

I didn't give a flip about the lip gloss. I'd kiss Dylan any day, for any reason. He was gentle, almost reverent, his fingertips holding my chin in place as his lips claimed me.

"Are you ready to go?" he asked when the kiss ended. I smiled up at him, suddenly a little shy. Unzipping my purse I said, "Almost." I dashed into the bathroom and made a quick repair to my lips before re-joining Dylan. I was heading to the door when he stopped me with a hand on my arm.

"One more thing," he said.

He picked up a velvet-covered box from the table beside him. My stomach pitched with nerves and apprehension. All of these clothes were one thing, but jewelry was another entirely.

I knew that the necklace and earrings I wore with the dress weren't sophisticated enough. My pearls were okay, but I was wearing Oscar de la Renta. A simple strand of cheap pearls didn't cut it.

Still, anything Dylan had in that box would be far more extravagant than what was appropriate. The dress alone went beyond the realm of acceptable gifts from a man I'd known only a day. Reading my mind, he said,

"Don't be stubborn."

"Dylan, you can't -"

"And don't tell me what to do. That was the deal. I'm

your date for the weekend, and in exchange, you're mine. That means you do what I say. No arguing."

"If you don't want any arguing, you've got the wrong girl," I said.

"I've got exactly the right girl," he said, opening the black velvet box to reveal a thick gold choker that gleamed in the evening light. Beside it sat matching earrings and bracelet. "I was tempted to go for diamonds. But those are for tomorrow's dress. This one calls for gold."

"When did you even have time to get these?" I asked, standing frozen as he fastened the choker around my neck. Without protest I took the earrings he handed me and began to put them in.

"I remembered them from the display downstairs. I had them delivered." Stepping back he surveyed me from head to toe, eyes hot and satisfied.

"You look like a goddess. Not that it matters, but your bitchy sisters are going to choke with envy when they see how gorgeous you are." He took my arm and drew me towards the door.

"That shows what you know," I said. "With sisters, it always matters."

"Not with those two. They should be beneath your notice, Leigha. Until they appreciate you for who you are, they aren't worthy of your attention."

I needed to write some of this down. When Dylan was out of my life, I could pull out his outrageous flattery to prop up my sagging ego. No man had ever seen me the way he did—as if I was special, extraordinary, exactly as I was.

Not sure what to say in response, I followed him to the elevator in silence. We stood together, side by side, my hand in his. Casually, he leaned down and whispered in my ear.

"You know that I have cameras everywhere in the Delecta."

I nodded. I knew that there were cameras everywhere in Vegas, not just at the Delecta.

"If there weren't, you'd be on your knees right now, sucking me with that sweet mouth until I filled it up. And you'd do it, wouldn't you? Just because I asked."

I nodded again. I couldn't lie. If the cameras hadn't been there, and he'd asked me to, I would have done it. Gone to my knees right there in the elevator. I might have done it even knowing the cameras were there if he'd asked.

In the last twenty-four hours, I hadn't had a good track record at saying no to Dylan. Just the thought of sucking his cock while the camera watched had my knees weak.

"You'd do it because you'd want to. Because deep down, you know you can trust me. That I'll take care of you, in every way you need or want."

Once more I nodded even though this time I had no idea what he meant. Did I know I could trust him? In some ways, I did.

In others, I was terrified to put my trust in any man, especially so soon after my ex had stolen so much from me. And what did he mean that he'd take care of me? Did he mean he'd make me come if I sucked him off? I had no doubt about that. So far every pleasure I'd given Dylan had been paid back twice over.

But what if he meant more than that? Thinking of the clothes and the jewelry, I wondered if he was talking about something bigger than sex. I pushed the thought away. Sex with Dylan was a dream. I wasn't fool enough to hope for more.

CHAPTER EIGHTEEN

DYLAN

I was in over my head with this girl. Half of the shit that came out of my mouth with her was unplanned. That wasn't me. I thought things through. I was methodical, calculating, and I always got my way.

With Leigha, I felt like I was struggling my way upstream, off balance and never getting as far as I wanted. I'd known her barely a day, and it felt like years.

She fit with me. Maybe not on the outside, but where it counted. This afternoon was a prime example. My plan had been simple. Eat, fuck some more, shower, get dressed, go to the rehearsal dinner, then bring her home and fuck her again and again.

Instead, we'd ended up sitting at the table talking about our work. My lust for her hadn't gone away--in fact it had been steadily growing since the last time I'd had her late that morning. But I'd found myself caught up in our conversation.

I'll admit, I started out wanting to impress her when I

told her what I did every day as one of the heads of Kane Enterprises.

But, she was genuinely interested in how I ran the business. Her questions were both curious and insightful, a compelling combination. Her passion for her own work was equally appealing.

I never thought I'd say that hearing the details of an accountant's nine to five would have me riveted. I should have been fighting sleep. That was Leigha, turning everything I thought I knew on its head.

Yes, she was gorgeous. That was a given. Call me shallow, but I'd never been drawn to ugly women. She was curvier than the current standard of beauty, sure, but she fit my standards to perfection. That she had a sharp brain was an unexpected bonus.

I'd gone into this looking for something different than my usual, but still, no more than a weekend fuck. The way I'd had to talk her into the whole thing had been half the fun, at first.

I liked that she wasn't another easy conquest, that she wanted me but wasn't ready to spread her legs just because I was reasonably attractive and rich. I was something special for her. It really hadn't occurred to me that she would end up being the same for me.

The change hadn't hit me until she'd tried to leave that morning. At the sight of her, teary eyed and edging for the door, panic had seized my chest. Fuck that. I never panicked, not over business, not over my life. Not the time Axel, Sam, and I were caught in a flash flood camping in the desert. And not ever over a woman.

Yet there I'd been, commanding her to stay while my heart pounded at the thought that she'd walk out. What the hell was wrong with me?

Leigha was different; I'd figured that out. And she was a seriously hot fuck. No question, the best I'd had despite her lack of experience—or maybe because of it, but it didn't matter. She was just a woman. There were thousands of those, beautiful and available, right outside my front door.

Why was this one so important? She thought I was a cheater? *Fine, then get out.* That's what I should have said. Instead, I'd soothed her, kissed her, and taken her to breakfast. All the while refusing to give her back her purse.

Keeping her purse was edging into stalker territory. She didn't need her wallet since I was paying for everything. Ditto on her keys, since we were taking my car. They were all excuses. Stealing a woman's purse and holding it hostage to keep her from leaving was nuts.

That brought me back to everything being upside down. Normally it was a challenge to scrape these girls off. I'd trapped Leigha so she couldn't leave me. Because I needed time for what? To fuck her until I got her out of my system? Or to convince her to stay?

CHAPTER NINETEEN

LEIGHA

I'd love to say that seeing my sisters' jaws drop at the sight of me didn't give me a rush. To say that I was mature and confident all on my own, without the dress and jewelry, without Dylan on my arm. That I didn't need to feel, for just one night, like I had the upper hand after years as the butt of their jokes. But I'd be lying. I'm not Mother Theresa.

Knowing that I was wearing more than they'd ever be able to afford, and I looked fantastic in it, felt like a victory after years of their cruel taunts. Never mind that I couldn't afford it either.

My heart was getting all tangled up with Dylan, but that didn't mean I couldn't appreciate that the point of our arrangement was working out better than I'd hoped. I didn't just have a date for the wedding, Dylan had turned me into a princess.

A princess who had her mind in the gutter. While I was greeting the other guests, nodding along to introductions and shaking hands, I was acutely aware of Dylan's hand on my back, the heat of his palm occasionally dipping low enough to cup my ass.

The dinner was a moment of triumph and all I wanted was to get back to the room and peel away every scrap of Dylan's tux so I could get my hands on the man beneath.

Now that I'd gotten to know him, I didn't want to waste our time together on this stupid wedding. Knowing my sister, she'd be getting married again in a few years. I'd never get another chance at a man like Dylan.

The cocktail hour was a blur of cheek kisses and polite hugs until we made our way over to Christie and Peter. They stood in the back of the room beside my mother, holding court as if they were visiting royalty.

I smiled at my mother when she caught sight of me. Her eyes went comically wide before she called out my name and rushed forward, enveloping me in a tight hug.

We were so different, my mom and me. She was bright colors and exuberance while I was understated and quiet. But wrapped in her tight embrace, the strong and familiar scent of her perfume in a cloud around us, my eyes got wet.

"You look so gorgeous, baby. Like a dream." She pulled back to cup my face in her hands, her eyes on mine, beaming with adoring love. "My beautiful girl."

Yep, no matter that we might be total opposites, I loved my Mom. Leaning in to kiss her cheek, I said, "You look great, too, Mom." She really did. Her little black dress had an emphasis on the 'little' and her cleavage was the opposite, but she looked great, especially considering she was the mother of three grown daughters.

She tugged me to her side, separating me from Dylan, who was promptly claimed by Christie and Cathie. He sent me a wink before turning to them.

Oddly, I wasn't worried about him being alone with my

sisters. From the things he'd said earlier and the night before, he despised them and liked me. Nothing those two harpies could say would change that.

"Did he take you shopping?" my Mom half-whispered into my ear. She'd backed us a few feet from the crowd so we could talk in relative privacy. I knew what she was getting at. Barbara Carmichael (I still couldn't get my brain to adjust to any of her more recent last names) knew clothes.

Depending on her current husband, she didn't always have the budget to shop as well as she'd like to, but she always knew the latest collections. So I wasn't the least bit surprised when she said, "I know that dress. De la Renta, from two months ago. And those sandals are Rene Caovilla's. I tried them on at Saks. He's not shying away from spending money on you."

"Mom, this isn't what you think. Don't get your hopes up."

"Leigha, no man spends twelve thousand dollars on a woman's clothes if he's planning on walking away. Trust me."

I choked on my champagne. Twelve thousand dollars? I'd known the dress and shoes had to be expensive, but that was insane. And she didn't know about the jewelry. As if she'd read my mind, she said,

"My guess is that necklace and the matching earrings and bracelet are his work as well. I'd give you an estimate on those, but I don't want you to pass out in the middle of your sister's rehearsal dinner."

"Mom," I whispered, "Stop. Seriously. You're freaking me out. I don't want to think about this."

"Well, you need to. That man looks at you as if he wants to protect you from everyone in the world except him. Pay attention and don't let him get away."

"Mom, really -" I stopped when she raised her hand in front of my face. Did she just give me the hand?

"Leigha, just keep your eyes open. That's all I'm saying. Men like Dylan don't come along every day. I should know." She glanced across the room at Christie and Cathie.

"Now I'm going to go save your man from your sisters before they scare him away. I swear, he looks like he wants to kill them already. I love all my girls, honey, but your sisters could try the patience of a saint."

With that, she walked away, her perfume trailing behind her. I meant to follow, but I was still reeling from everything she'd said. Twelve thousand dollars. Not counting the gold I wore around my neck, my ears and on my wrist.

I'd been agonizing about Steven stealing ten grand and Dylan had dropped more than that in one day, just on clothes I didn't even need. Adding in the other evening dress, shoes, dresses, and lingerie, I didn't want to even want to try to guess how much he'd spent.

It was probably enough to pay off half my mortgage. I didn't know what to think about that. Was my mother right? Was he planning to be with me past the weekend?

It would make sense. A man didn't head a corporation worth billions by being careless with money and throwing away this much cash on a weekend fling would be crazy. Still, the thought of being with Dylan longer term was hard to take in. Things like that didn't happen to me.

I was so distracted, an arm slid around my waist before I noticed anyone nearby. I didn't have to look up to know it wasn't Dylan. The bad cologne was enough to clue me in. Peter. I tried to ease away without causing a scene, but his fingers tightened on my waist.

"You're looking uncharacteristically sexy tonight,

Leigha. Who knew you had it in you? You usually dress like an accountant."

"I am an accountant, Peter." I pulled back on his arm, trying to move away. His arm didn't give. Dipping his head to my cheek, he said, "Once the new guy gets tired of you, I'll be here. I can take care of you too, Leigha."

"You're marrying my sister," I hissed, leaning back. This guy was disgusting. How could my sister be marrying him?

"Christie is a practical woman. As long as I can keep her credit card bills paid, she doesn't ask questions."

I didn't want to draw attention, but I couldn't take another second of his slimy hands. As subtly as I could, I jammed the spike heel of my sparkly gold sandal into Peter's instep. His arm loosened, and I stepped away, trying not to cringe at the trail of his fingertips along my waist. Yuck.

"Don't be so rude, Leigha," he chided, only slightly favoring his foot as he stepped back. "When this guy dumps you, you'll be on your own. I could be a good friend."

"Fuck off, Peter."

Not an original come back, but I was too grossed out to be witty. I whirled around, just wanting to get away from him.

The sad thing was, I believed him about Christie. Not that she'd be cool with me being her husband's mistress, but that she didn't ask too many questions. I wondered how many late meetings and business trips he had. I was betting it was a lot.

The thought depressed me. I didn't really like my sister, but she was my sister. A marriage of convenience with Peter wasn't a happy prospect.

This time when an arm wound around my waist, I

relaxed into it, recognizing Dylan by instinct, even before his clean, masculine scent hit me.

"Sorry you got stuck with the evil twins while I talked to my Mom," I said.

"That's okay. You can make it up to me later." The promise in his voice was enough to heat my blood. "What did Peter want?" he asked.

"Nothing." No way was I going to tell Dylan what Peter had said. I had a feeling he wouldn't take it well. And Peter wasn't worth pissing Dylan off. I could handle Peter.

"I didn't like him touching you," Dylan said, his mouth moving against my ear in a whisper of a kiss.

"Neither did I," I admitted.

"You're mine. No one touches you but me. Understood?"

"Dylan," I said, pulling away so I could face him. "I didn't want him to touch me. I got rid of him as fast as I could."

"I know." Dylan took my hips in his hands and tugged me against him. Dipping his head to mine, he said, "I know you didn't like it. And I know you were being polite. Next time, don't be. No one touches you but me. Ever. That's more important than being polite. Now tell me you understand."

"What if I don't want *you* to touch me?" I couldn't help asking. Dylan nipped my ear, his teeth drawing a flash of pain that turned immediately into heat.

"If you don't want me to touch you, we've got bigger problems than your fuck-head of a brother in law getting in your face."

"Okay." That was the best I could come up with. My brain had scattered at the touch of his teeth to my ear.

"Good. He touches you again, he answers to me."

"Okay." My brain clicked back into gear. "If it bothers you so much, why did you leave me with him?"

"I wanted to see what you would do," Dylan said. I lurched back, suddenly pissed off.

"What?" I screeched. He'd left me to handle that pig as a *test*? Dylan's arms tightened, not letting me move. People turned their heads to look.

Dylan grinned down at me and pressed a kiss to my temple, whispering,"I'm buying you ten more pairs of heels just like that. I wouldn't be surprised to see him leaving tracks of blood. You did a good job, sweetheart."

I didn't want to, but I melted—not just at him calling me sweetheart, but his praise. Testing me was high-handed and annoying. His being proud of me was hard to resist.

Before I could think of what to say, Peter announced that it was time to go into dinner. Good. One meal, and hopefully not too many speeches to get through, and I'd be alone with Dylan again.

CHAPTER TWENTY

Dylan and I checked the seating chart on an easel by the door and found we were seated in the far end of the room, furthest from the wedding party. I knew Christie had stuck us there to make a point.

As her sister, I should have been sitting close to her, Cathie, and my mother. For the first time, I was thrilled she was a spiteful bitch. I'd rather be alone in a corner with Dylan than sitting near the wedding party any day.

Dylan pulled my chair out for me and helped me sit before taking his own seat. No one sat to his left. On my left was an older couple I didn't recognize.

After stilted introductions, during which Dylan neglected to mention his last name, the couple turned to face the rest of the table and ignored us. Perfect. If we drowned out the sound of one of the groomsmen getting ready to give a speech, we could almost pretend we were alone.

We both stayed quiet and ate our salad while the groomsmen droned on and on about his long friendship with Peter. About anyone else, it might have been sweet. But since I knew he was talking about Peter, it was mostly annoying.

I zoned out a little, trying to enjoy the meal and wondering how long it would take, when I felt the weight of Dylan's hand on my leg.

Trying not to be obvious, I looked up at him. Dylan's eyes were on the speaking groomsman, his expression bland and vaguely interested. For all that anyone else could see, he was the picture of innocence. Beneath the table, his fingers slipped beneath my skirt and trailed along the sensitive skin of my inner thigh.

"Dylan," I hissed. His eyes flicked to me and he winked, then went back to pretending to pay attention to the speech. That was my only effort at protest. Why bother? By now I knew Dylan would do what he wanted to.

Whatever he wanted to do was guaranteed to be more fun for me than sitting here and acting like I cared about the rehearsal dinner.

Adjusting my napkin so that it more fully hid the movement of Dylan's hand between my legs, I dropped my eyes to my plate and shut out all the other diners.

He teased me, trailing his fingertips in figure eights up and down my leg, the side of his hand brushing innocuously against my delicate lace panties. I tried to act like he wasn't driving me crazy, like I couldn't feel the heat build between my legs with every pass of his fingers.

I just wasn't that cool. When he brushed against my panties one more time, I barely caught myself before I moaned. The man beside me shifted, as if he was going to look at me, then my silence convinced him it wasn't worth the effort.

I sank my teeth into my lower lip and slid down a little in the high backed chair, opening my left leg toward Dylan.

No change. Only more of those teasing, light touches. I could feel myself getting wet. If I thought he would let me get away with it, I would have jumped out of my chair and dragged Dylan to the nearest coat closet.

Somehow, I didn't think I could pull that off. This was Dylan's game, and if I didn't play by his rules, I'd lose. Since winning with Dylan meant an unbelievable orgasm, I didn't want to lose. But maybe I could get a little creative.

Curious to see what he'd do, I slipped my hand into his lap. Beneath the dark wool of his suit, he was hard. I closed my hand around his length and squeezed.

He gave a slight jerk in his chair before calmly putting down his soup spoon and removing my hand from his lap. Tilting his head in my direction, he said, under his breath,

"No."

"If you can, why can't I?" A long, intent look, dripping with meaning. Okay, I knew why. But still...

"You're making me insane," I murmured. "Are you going to do this all through dinner?"

The thought was both enticing and horrifying. We were only on the soup course, and groomsmen number two was rambling on and on about some team he and Peter were on in college. Barring a natural disaster or foreign invasion, we could be here for hours. While Christie might not care if we snuck out, my mother would.

"That depends," he asked. "Do you really want me to stop?"

"No. I want you to keep going." At the aggravation in my voice, he grinned.

"Take off your panties, and I'll give you what you want." His voice was so low I barely heard him.

"Here?"

"Right here."

I didn't answer. How was I going to get my underwear off in the middle of the dining room? We were at the far end of the room. The light was dim. But, I had a man sitting just to my right.

Dylan was crazy. He wouldn't make me come unless I figured out how to get my undies off while I was still sitting here, with barely the edge of the tablecloth to cover what I was doing. My pride wanted me to turn down his challenge. My body wanted the orgasm he would give me if I obeyed his ridiculous challenge.

"Excuse me," I said under my breath to the man beside me. Fortunately, he didn't spare me more than a quick glance.

Twisting in my seat so that I faced Dylan, I lifted my left hip off the chair and reached beneath my skirt. The high-low hem was my friend as there wasn't much skirt to get out of the way.

Tagging the edge of my panties, I hooked my index finger in the fabric and gave a sharp pull, dragging them down below my ass. A good start, but that was the easy side.

Pretending I hadn't done anything out of the ordinary, I took a spoonful of soup. I went to put the spoon down beside the plate and dropped it on the floor instead. It was too obvious, but I couldn't think of anything else. Nudging my seat back a few inches, I murmured,

"Excuse me. Sorry." I eased my seat back a little more and leaned forward as if reaching for the floor. The second my head was below the table, I lifted my rear-end off the seat and reached beneath my skirt for the other side of my panties, using my napkin to cover the sight of my hand going up my own skirt.

From beside me, I heard Dylan clear his throat. My head popped up, and to my horror, I saw the servers coming to clear the soup course, starting at the ends of the tables.

In a panic, I gave the panties one more tug before sitting back up and scooting my chair into place. I made it just in time to sit back and let a uniformed server remove my bowl.

"Did you find your spoon, sweetheart?" Dylan asked, a devilish twinkle in his eyes.

I scowled back at him. I wasn't actually all that annoyed. The potential disaster of getting caught taking off my underwear in public was turning me on. I'd wanted my orgasm before, but now I really wanted it.

That pleasure was mine, Dylan was going to give it to me, and all I had to do was take off my underwear without leaving the table. I wasn't going to get caught. I was going to do what Dylan told me to and then I was going to come.

I was so close. My panties were still on, but I'd managed to get them around my thighs. I knew without asking that it wasn't enough. If Dylan said he wanted them off, they were going to come off.

This time, I waited until the servers were finished clearing the soup before I made my last move. Smoothing my napkin across my lap, I twisted the skirt beneath over to the side so I could reach my left hand beneath the hem.

The man on my right never noticed as I lifted my thighs an inch and pulled the panties to my knees. From there it was only a wiggle to get the scrap of fabric to fall to the floor. I'd have to remember to pick them up before we left.

I'd chosen the almost transparent black lace from among the pieces Dylan had bought that afternoon. All of them were La Perla and all gorgeous. I wasn't abandoning this pair under the table.

With a self-satisfied smirk at Dylan, I reclined in the

seat and let my knees fall apart. My napkin was still spread across my lap, shielding Dylan's hand from view as it slid beneath my hem, then up between my parted thighs.

I bit my lip in anticipation and fixed my face in a polite smile, pretending I was listening to Christie's best friend from high school rhapsodizing about cheer squad as if she hadn't given the same speech at Christie's first wedding just a few years before.

Dylan didn't make me wait. Instead of teasing me with endless, light strokes, he went straight for the good stuff. A breath after he touched my thigh, his fingertips grazed my clit. I fought back a shudder, all my effort going into hiding my response to his touch.

He pressed the swollen bead of flesh, watching for my reaction before he pinched it between two fingers and squeezed. I think I jumped. I know I made a tiny squeaking sound, startling the man beside me. He looked at my face for a moment before turning his eyes back to the brides-maid's speech.

My attention was completely divided between the need for silence and my rising arousal. I'd already been hot from Dylan touching my leg. Taking off my panties without being seen by the rest of the guests had only made me hotter.

Now Dylan's fingers played between my legs, toying with my clit and spreading my slick heat in circles around my entrance. I wanted to come, wanted to scream with orgasm right there in the packed dining room. I'd have to keep my mouth shut and my body still or risk total humiliation.

I sank my teeth into my bottom lip and breathed through my nose, deep, even breaths like I'd take in yoga class. Quiet and calm. At complete odds with the building need in my pussy.

Silent and frozen, my entire consciousness narrowed to the splinters of sharp, bright pleasure between my legs. The strength and heat of Dylan's hand. His fingers pressing, rotating, dipping inside.

I rocked my hips in a tiny, experimental motion. The flare of pleasure was dizzying, but the slide of my chair told me I couldn't do it again. I'd have to remain passive, trusting Dylan to give me what I wanted.

In theory, that wasn't a problem. In reality, I wanted my orgasm now, not when Dylan decided I could have it. I turned my head to face him, meeting his intense green eyes. Fixed on my face, they were hot, demanding, and in control.

"Please," I whispered. "I'll do anything. Don't make me wait anymore." His eyes flared.

"Anything?" he asked. I don't know why I'd said that. With Dylan, it really could be 'anything'. I had no idea where his limits were, but it was a guarantee that they went much further than my own.

Who was I kidding? I'd done everything he'd demanded so far. My offer of 'anything' was a joke. I'd do what he wanted anyway, even if that included waiting for my orgasm, or not coming at all. So far, doing what he asked had brought me more pleasure than I'd ever imagined.

"Anything," I said under my breath.

Dylan's eyes went the deep green of a forest at twilight as he drove two fingers into my pussy. It took everything I had to stop my gasp at the sensation of finally being full after so much teasing.

I would have preferred his cock to his fingers, but even overcome with need I wasn't crazy enough to consider fucking him in the dining room.

As turned on as I was, it wouldn't take much more before the rising orgasm swept me under. His arm in the perfect position, Dylan moved his fingers in short, pulsing thrusts as he pressed the heel of his hand into my clit.

Pure, exalted bliss exploded in my brain and washed through my body, locking my muscles in place. I didn't move, but I heard myself give a tiny whimper. I don't know if anyone heard, and I didn't care.

When the last wave of pleasure faded, I came back to myself, noticing that Dylan's hand was back in his own lap and my skirt was pulled neatly down beneath my napkin. Reveling in sated relaxation, I turned to look at Dylan.

His grin said he was pretty satisfied with himself. The bulge in his suit pants said he might have been emotionally satisfied, but his body still wanted more.

A feeling of dread pushed out my calm. I'd said *anything*. What was he going to ask me to do?

CHAPTER TWENTY-ONE

LEIGHA

I had two choices. I could pretend I didn't know I owed him one and eat my dinner. Or I could bite the bullet and find out what the payback would be.

I was shy, but I wasn't a wimp. At least, I didn't want to be. I didn't want to return Dylan's generosity by being afraid of him. He'd said I could trust him.

"So," I said, trying for casual, "What's my *anything*?"

He didn't answer right away, just looked at me, reading my eyes. He probably saw everything. My vulnerability, my nerves, my need to please him. I could only hope he'd take it easy on me.

When he continued to stare in silence, I fought the urge to look away. I wanted Dylan. Wanted to be worthy of the powerful, vibrant man he was. He wanted me to submit to him, but I sensed he wanted a woman who could hold her own against his strong personality. I needed to find a way to do both.

Finally, he smiled a gentle, unexpectedly sweet smile.

Dipping his head into mine, he laid a soft kiss on my mouth. Leaning in a little closer, he said,

"Your *anything* is for later. I'm saving it. For now, just enjoy the rest of dinner."

"You're sure?" I asked, not quite able to believe he was letting me off this easy. I'd had visions of under the table blow jobs or sneaking off to find an unoccupied closet. Neither of which I really wanted to do.

"Eat," he said, gesturing with his fork to my untouched dinner plate. Remembering my post-orgasmic inattention when the servers had delivered it, I flushed. Oh, well. If they'd seen anything amiss, there was nothing I could do about it now.

Christie had ordered filet mignon, asparagus and some kind of potato dish with a creamy sauce. Yum. Taking Dylan's suggestion, I dug in.

The rest of the meal passed in a blur of more boring speeches made tolerable by the delicious food, excellent wine, and Dylan beside me. We were silent, but I was acutely aware of his presence.

At one point, between the removal of our dinner plates and dessert, Dylan reached out and took my hand in his. I expected him to drop it in his lap, or start a conversation, but he did neither. He just held my hand, playing with my fingertips. When I caught his eye, he winked.

He had my head spinning. Just when I thought this was all about sex, he did something so sweet I was tempted to hope it was more.

I'd held hands with men before and felt nothing from it, but this was different—maybe because it was Dylan. He wasn't teasing me or trying to turn me on. He was keeping me close. It was dangerous. Not for him, for me.

I wasn't the kind of girl to have casual sex. I wished I

were. Life would be so much simpler if I could be like some of my friends, going out to clubs on the weekend to find a guy and get laid. I'd tried it, but it had felt wrong.

Either I'd liked the guy and ended up feeling used, or I was just attracted to him, and I regretted it later. So I knew myself well enough to understand that, as much as I'd like him to be, Dylan wasn't an exception. I was falling hard for him.

And it wasn't the clothes, the jewelry, or the orgasms. It was him. His strength, and the combination of power and gentleness, the way he could be demanding and then sweet. How he wanted me to follow his orders, but he was thinking of me the whole time.

How could I resist falling for a man like this? I couldn't. Every time I got a hint that I wasn't just a weekend fling, my hungry heart ate it up. I was heading for disaster. I knew it. I couldn't stop myself.

The servers made a last trip in with dessert and coffee. One more course, and we could escape. Fortunately, the wedding party was finished with their speeches. Another one of those and I would have fallen asleep at the table.

Dylan and I both started on our chocolate torts with raspberry sauce. I sipped my coffee, trying to offset the glasses of wine I'd had with dinner. I didn't know what the rest of the night would bring, but I didn't want to be tired.

Putting down my fork, I pushed back my chair. Some of the guests had gotten up to wander around and socialize. I had to find the ladies room, and this seemed like the most inconspicuous time to do it

After my (hopefully silent) orgasm at the table, I hadn't wanted to draw any more attention to myself than necessary.

"I'll be right back," I said to Dylan, picking up my purse

so I could refresh my lip gloss. Dylan narrowed his eyes and nodded.

The ladies room was down a long hall outside the entrance to the private dining room. I expected it to be crowded, but there was only one other woman in there, an older lady I didn't recognize.

I did what I had to and spent a few minutes fixing my lips and adjusting my hair, pleased to see that even without panties, and after a mind blowing orgasm, I still looked pretty damn good.

I was feeling satisfied with myself right up until I pushed open the bathroom door and ran into Peter. The men's bathroom was down the hall and there was no one else in the ladies, so he could only be waiting for me.

Wary, I tried to edge around him. He shifted to block me and grabbed my wrist. A hard yank on my arm wasn't enough to shake him off. I lifted a foot to go after his instep again, but he jerked on my arm, knocking me off balance.

In my sparkly, stiletto heel sandals, it was impossible to dig in and resist when he pulled me into the shadows down the hall.

"Relax," he said, tugging me closer to him. "I just want to talk to you."

"I don't think we have anything to say."

"I think we do. You misunderstood me earlier."

This, I had to hear. Was he going to apologize? Or demonstrate that he was even more of a pig than I thought?

"Leigha," he said, tugging me closer.

His breath smelled like sour coffee. It was an improvement over his cologne. My nose rebelled, and I tried to breathe through my mouth. How could Christie stand him? He was rich, and she loved money, but couldn't she find someone less repellant to marry?

"I know you're wondering how my proposal would work, with you here in Vegas and me in Chicago. But you don't have to worry about that. I have a new contract that means I'll be in Vegas all the time. We'll hook up while I'm here, and no one will ever know."

"Are you serious?"

"Do you think I can't take care of you? Once Kane is done fucking you, you'll want another sugar daddy. Why not me?" Peter raked me with his eyes, taking me in from my breasts to my toes. He didn't bother looking at my face.

"I didn't think you had it in you," he went on. "You always dressed in those frumpy clothes, I had no idea what you were hiding under there. Your tits alone - "

I jerked back on my arm again, too disgusted to worry about losing my balance. Peter was too offensive to listen to a second longer. I no longer cared if I caused a scene.

What gave him the right to treat me like a piece of meat just because I was dressed up for once? And what about my sister? Calling him a pig was an insult to swine.

Peter tightened his hold on my arm, refusing to let me go. He opened his mouth, probably to say something else insulting, and I couldn't help myself. I was in the wrong position to jab him with my heels, but I still had one free arm. Without thinking, I swung my fist at his face.

At the pop of my fist against his nose, Peter yelped and reeled back. What he didn't do was let go of me. As I teetered in my sandals, losing my balance as his grip on my arm jerked me back and forth, an arm came around my waist, steadying me. Dylan. Relief flooded through me.

I wasn't a fighter. That punch was the best I had in my arsenal. If things had gotten ugly, I would have thought of something, but Dylan could handle Peter better than I could. I knew my strengths, and beating up guys wasn't one of them.

With a stiff chop of one hand, Dylan struck at Peter's arm just above his wrist. Abruptly, and with another yelp, Peter let me go. Dylan took advantage of Peter's whining over his wrist to slide me to the side, out of the way.

"Sorry I took so long," he said. "I almost missed him sneaking out of the dining room."

"It's okay. You're here now." Looking up into his angry green eyes, I said, "I punched him." Dylan grinned at me, still pissed, and now amused. It was an intoxicating expression.

"I see that," he said, kissing me on the tip of my nose. Sweet again. He was killing me. "Do you mind if I have a word with him?"

I shook my head, suspecting that Dylan's plan involved speaking with a part of his anatomy other than his mouth. Peter finally dropped his wrist and stared at Dylan.

"What's your problem? Leigha and I were just talking."

I could guess what Dylan was thinking. Something along the lines of Peter not touching me ever again. He didn't bother explaining his position to Peter. Instead, he hauled off and swung.

Peter's nose was already dribbling blood from my punch. With Dylan's, his face exploded red. It would have been gross if it hadn't been Peter. I wasn't a fan of physical violence, but Peter had it coming. Dylan hit him again, this time on the chin. Peter stumbled back until he hit the wall. His feet went out from under him and he slid to the floor in an ungainly sprawl. One trembling hand touched his nose.

"You broke my nose," he sputtered, his voice muffled, as if he had a head cold. Dylan shrugged in disinterest.

"I'll sue your ass off. You can't do this to me. Do you know who I am?"

At that, Dylan laughed.

"No. But I know who *I* am. Go ahead, press charges. This hallway is under surveillance. You're in *my* casino, asswipe. You assaulted one of *my* guests, who happens to be my girlfriend. Not only should you rethink pressing charges, I suggest you make up a good explanation for your fiancée on the way to the hospital to get that nose looked at."

Did he call me his girlfriend? He did. Was it because it was easier and sounded more normal than calling me his lover? Or because he meant it? And if he meant it, what did that mean? My head reeling, I didn't protest when Dylan took my hand and tugged me closer, tucking me into his side as we went down the hall.

"I don't think we'll go back to the party," he said. I shook my head in agreement. As soon as we were clear of the restaurant and back in the casino proper, Dylan stopped and turned me to face him. "Let me see that hand."

He lifted my hand and studied my knuckles. I hadn't noticed until that moment, but my hand hurt. My knuckles were tender, the skin scraped on two of them. I hadn't realized I'd hit Peter that hard. Dylan stroked my fingers and said,

"This is going to bruise. Let's get you some ice."

We were walking to a nearby bar, when I heard from behind me,

"Dylan, hold up."

As one, we turned around to see two men coming toward us. Both tall, both heart stoppingly gorgeous. I was all Dylan's, no question. But these two were perfect specimens of male beauty.

One with short, dark hair, his eyes so deep a brown they

were almost black, dressed in a suit much like Dylan's. The other blond, eyes a bright blue, in a more casual button down shirt and jacket. They came to a stop in front of us and looked me over. The blond one said,

"So this is who you stood us up for? Nice."

Dylan scowled back at them.

CHAPTER TWENTY-TWO

DYLAN

F uck. I should have known those bastards would be up to something. Sam had taken it too well when I'd called to cancel our plans. They were my closest friends, good guys, loyal to the end.

I wanted them nowhere near Leigha. She was too tempting, and they were both dogs. So was I, but that wasn't the point. Leigha was mine. I planned to introduce her to Sam and Axel eventually, but not yet.

Not until things were more solid between us. Half the time she acted like she was completely into me. The rest of the time, she looked like she was getting ready to bolt.

"What are you guys doing here?" I asked, aware I sounded annoyed and surly. Sam grinned. Axel raised his dark eyebrows. Fuck. They were going to be annoying. The three of us were best friends, but in the way of males everywhere, we never missed an opportunity to give each other shit. Apparently, it was my turn.

"Looking for you," Sam said, his grin widening further

when I glared at him. "Aren't you going to introduce us to your very attractive friend?" He winked at Leigha.

My adrenaline was still high from hitting Peter, my body on alert for any threat to my woman. In my head I knew it was just Sam fucking with me. I still couldn't help the growl in the back of my throat. Before I could stop her, Leigha reached out her hand.

"I'm Leigha Carmichael."

"Sam Logan." He took her hand in his and shook it. She winced. Irritation flared inside me. I snatched her hand back and examined it.

"Introductions are over. This is Leigha. Leigha, the silent one is Axel. You met Sam. Now we're getting ice for your hand."

Fortunately for my temper, she didn't protest when I took her uninjured hand and dragged her toward the nearest bar. Yes, I was acting like a Neanderthal. No, I couldn't help it.

I'd let my woman get in a situation where she had to punch a scumbag to protect herself. I was proud of her for fighting back, but she shouldn't have had to. I should have been on top of it. I didn't have time to deal with Sam and Axel. They fell into step on either side of us.

"How did she hurt her hand?" Axel asked, taking a side-long look at Leigha's hand.

"Punched an asshole," I said.

"Where were you?" Axel's brow was raised again, partly in curiosity, mostly in censure. I didn't need it. I knew I was responsible.

"Following him. Too slowly, it turned out."

"Dylan, I'm okay," Leigha interrupted. "Really. I've been wanting to punch Peter for months. If you'd shown up earlier, I'd have missed my chance."

That was my girl, trying to give me what I needed. I had no doubt Leigha had enjoyed hitting that fucker, but she shouldn't have had to. We reached the bar and claimed a row of high-backed stools.

"A bag of ice for the lady's hand," I said to the bartender. He nodded and disappeared into the back.

"So you ditched us for a girl," Sam said, shaking his head. To Leigha, he said, "What are you doing with this guy? Why don't you give me a shot and see what I can do for you?"

To my right I saw Axel shake his head. Sam was the funny one of the three of us. I opened my mouth to tell him to shut the fuck up when Leigha spoke, her voice caught in a laugh, light and sweet.

"You might want to rethink that offer. I punched the last guy who tried to get me away from Dylan."

Sam winced and pretended to duck his head in fear of her fists. Axel smiled and shook his head again. He knew me well enough to hold back the teasing until I'd at least taken care of Leigha's hand. So did Sam, but he was always willing to test my temper if he thought it was funny.

"Did you leave the guy alive?" Axel asked, only half kidding. I shrugged.

"Yeah. But he's not going to look too pretty at his wedding." Leigha giggled.

"Christie is going to be so pissed. Even if his nose isn't broken, he'll look awful. He was bleeding everywhere."

At Sam and Axel's confused look, she said, "Christie is my sister. I'm here for her wedding. Peter is the groom. And Dylan and I met when I was crying into my drink because I didn't have a date for the wedding. He came to my rescue."

"I can't imagine you didn't have men lined up out the door to take you out," Sam said, dropping his jokester persona for the smooth charm he used on women. He'd better check that with Leigha. I'd taken him down before. I'd do it again if I had to. Leigha just smiled at him and shook her head.

"I live a quiet life," she said in explanation. "So, you three are friends? Do you guys work with Dylan?"

"No," I said, cutting in. "Sam owns Desert Vistas Construction and Axel is the western head of Sinclair Security. I contract with him on occasion." Leigha looked from Sam to Axel to me.

"Okay. Wow. I know both of those companies. They're huge. So you're all billionaires? And you hang out together? You're like the Alpha Billionaire's Club. Talk about dates being lined up out the door." She looked at her feet, trying to hide her smile. "I might faint from the concentration of hotness."

Even Axel smiled at that. For someone who was shy by nature, Leigha was coming out of her shell. I approved of her growing confidence, even though I hated that she was using it to flirt with my friends.

The bartender returned with a plastic bag of crushed ice. I thanked him and took it, pressing it gently to Leigha's bruised knuckles. I knew my friends. They sensed Leigha wasn't one of my interchangeable dates and they weren't going to leave us alone until they got a feel for her. I might as well settle in and make the best of it.

CHAPTER TWENTY-THREE

LEIGHA

Dylan held the bag of ice against my hand with care, conscious that too much pressure would bring me pain. I could tell he was still riled up from the confrontation with Peter and pissed that I'd hurt myself.

I didn't care about my hand. A little pain was worth seeing Peter bleeding from my punch to his nose. What an ass. I couldn't believe my sister was really going to marry him. If she'd been a different woman, I'd have told her about Peter, tried to convince her to call it off.

Christie wouldn't care that he was planning to cheat. She'd probably spent the last month personally interviewing for their pool boy—very personally.

Dylan's free arm came around my waist, pulling me back until I was flush with his chest. Taking a deep breath, I relaxed into him. I didn't know what kind of cologne he wore, or if that scent was just his soap, but he always smelled so good.

He and his friends had changed the subject off me and

onto something else. I wasn't paying attention. Something about vandalism on a construction site.

Our small group drew eyes from all over the casino floor, mostly women checking out the three hot men at the bar. The way Dylan held me, I could barely be seen over his shoulder except by Sam, Axel, and the bartender.

That was fine with me. I'd had a little fun joking around with Dylan's friends, but I only wanted Dylan's attention. Funny how being with Dylan gave me the confidence to flirt with Sam and Axel.

Normally I wouldn't be able to work up the nerve to speak to men that attractive, but with Dylan at my side, knowing I was his, I was comfortable. The bartender returned and asked for our order.

"What do you want, love?" Dylan asked dipping his head to touch his lips to the shell of my ear. I shivered against him.

"Just water, please. Nothing more to drink."

"Good girl. I don't want you falling asleep on me."

He passed my order along to the bartender and went back to his discussion with Sam and Axel. I could have joined in. They weren't excluding me. But I was happy to be where I was, cuddled into Dylan, letting my mind drift over the rest of our evening.

So far, sex with Dylan had been demanding, mind-blowing, and unexpected. I was both nervous and eager to see what he had in store for me next.

I people watched, occasionally contributing to the conversation when I had something to say. In the time it took us to empty our glasses, three sets of women had come up to us and hit on the guys, Dylan included.

They didn't seem to care that he was glued to me. They propositioned him right over my head. Each time, he politely, yet firmly, pointed out that he was both taken, and not interested.

The fourth pair of predatory females was a cut above the others. I didn't know a lot of beautiful women, but these two were perfection. One a redhead and the other blonde, they were tall, shapely, and exquisitely dressed.

"Well, look who we found," the redhead said, winding her arm around Sam's waist. Clearly she knew the guys. The blonde winked at Dylan and kissed Axel on the cheek.

"My favorite troublemakers," she said. "It's a good thing Charity had other plans since you have your hands full," she said to Dylan. His arm around my waist squeezed tight. I wasn't sure if it was in possession or reassurance.

"I do," he answered. "Leigha, meet Lacey and Violet."

I didn't have my hands free since one was still on ice and the other was trapped by Dylan's arm, so I nodded and smiled. To my surprise, both women nodded and smiled back.

"Too bad for us," Violet said from her place beside Sam. Giving Sam a playful elbow in his gut, she went on, "Dylan is the best of these three."

"Hey," Sam said in affront. "You've never complained before."

"Not complaining, sweetie. Just pointing out that Dylan is the best catch of the three of you."

"Because of his business?" I asked, ready to change my cautious approval to dislike if Violet was judging Dylan on his bank account.

"Not that, honey. All three of these boys are loaded. But Sam is a terminal bachelor. Someday Axel and Dylan will both settle down, but not Sam."

"So what's wrong with me? Why is Dylan a better catch than I am?" Axel asked, not sounding the least bit concerned that he wasn't at the top of their list. Considering that Lacey was pressed up against him, he didn't seem to have cause for worry.

Lacey shot him a look that said, 'Get real.' Out loud, she said, "You're a little scary. So serious all the time. And your job isn't exactly low key."

"I thought you ran Sinclair Security?" I asked. Axel seemed serious, but I wouldn't have called him scary.

"I do," he said, a wry smile curving his lips. "But I also handle our more specialized cases."

"Sometimes they get a little hairy," Sam cut in.

"Oh," I said.

I could only imagine the kind of jobs Axel took. I'd heard of Sinclair Security. They didn't do pay-by-the-month house alarms. They specialized in elite systems for the wealthiest clients. And they provided personal security for everyone from visiting dignitaries to celebrities with scary stalkers.

I knew about them because one of their people had foiled an assassination attempt on a foreign ambassador a few months before. He'd foiled it by taking the bullet himself. It had been huge in the news. Not only had the Sinclair team protected their client, they'd tracked down the assassin and handed him over to the police.

I gave Axel another look. This time, I saw it. Beneath his quiet demeanor was a core of steel. This man would get the job done, no matter what it took. Curious, I asked,

"Was the ambassador's attempted assassination one of your hairy cases?" I knew he'd know what I was talking about. The assassination attempt had been on every news channel for over a week. Axel shook his head.

"The ambassador was business as usual. Unfortunate

that it hit the news. We like to keep a low profile. News should be about our clients, not our agents."

"Is the guy who got shot okay? The last I saw, he was in the hospital."

"He's back in the field. It was only a shoulder, nothing serious."

"Good," I said. Axel winked at me.

He was hot, no question. That thick, short, dark hair, his almost black eyes, a lean but powerful build. Still, Lacey was right. Not exactly great relationship material.

I sure as hell wouldn't be comfortable with a man who considered a bullet to the shoulder a minor issue. Not if he was out there facing far more dangerous stuff than just being shot.

The woman who took him on would have to be strong enough to handle his job and laid back enough not to freak out about it. Feeling like poking at him, I leaned my head back and looked up at Dylan.

"Your job isn't dangerous, is it?" He rubbed his chin against my temple, smiling down at me.

"Not remotely. Stressful sometimes. But not dangerous."

"Good," I whispered, forgetting for a moment that we had company. Dylan's eyes had darkened to a rich green, the color so deep I felt myself falling into them. His eyes were saying something I liked, something warm and hopeful that had my heart racing. A throat cleared. I flushed and looked up to see Axel studying me with a grave expression.

"That's what I'm talking about," Violet said, gesturing at Dylan and me.

"All right," Sam said. "Enough of that, Dyl. You're making us look bad in front of the ladies." Turning to Lacey and Violet, he said, "Do you two want to go out and have some fun? It looks like Dylan and Leigha are in for the night."

Both women agreed, and with a few nods and winks, the four of them left the bar. The ice bag on my knuckles was mostly water by this point. I dropped it on the bar beside my empty water glass.

"Do you want to go and have some fun?" Dylan asked.

"Only if the fun is upstairs in your penthouse," I said. "Your friends were nice, but I don't want to share you anymore."

His fierce smile was all the answer I needed. With one arm wrapped tightly around my shoulder, Dylan led the way to the elevators. This time, our silent ride up to the penthouse didn't leave me feeling awkward and uncertain. I thought I was coming to understand where I stood with Dylan. I hoped I was.

Without speaking, we passed through the entryway and into his penthouse. As soon as we crossed the threshold, Dylan turned and headed straight for the bedroom. I followed without protest.

In complete silence, he stopped beside the bed and stared at me, taking me in from head to toe. I stared back, absorbing the way he looked in his perfectly tailored suit, hoping it would shortly be on the floor. Reading my mind, he stripped off his jacket, dropping it on the bed. His shirt followed seconds later, his eyes never leaving mine.

I reached for the zipper at my back, lowering it slowly. When it was all the way down, I stopped, letting Dylan push the lace of the bodice off my shoulders. The fabric caught on my breasts before giving in to the pull of gravity and falling to the carpet. I stood there, naked except for my spike-heeled sandals. I expected Dylan to pounce. I was tempted to pounce on him, and he only had his shirt off.

What he did took me by surprise, melting my wary heart. Stepping closer, until the tips of my breasts touched his chest, he took my mouth in a slow, devastating kiss. His kiss didn't rush, didn't push. He tasted me—no, he *savored* me. I know, because I was doing the same - falling deeper and deeper into our kiss as my hands sank into his thick, silky hair.

We stood there kissing for what felt like forever. When he finally turned and lowered me to my back on the comforter, I was more than ready for him. But then, I'd been ready since before I'd unzipped my dress. I opened my legs, inviting him into my body, lifting my arms in welcome.

After the violence of the fight with Peter, and Dylan's anger that I was hurt, I expected his touch to be rough. Demanding. I wasn't prepared for tenderness. Dylan moved us up the bed until I was cradled in the pillows and fell to worshiping my body with determined focus.

His hands skated over my skin, stroking, rubbing, paying just as much attention to my rib cage and my elbows as he did to my breasts. He took his time, exploring every inch of me, lavishing attention all over.

I squirmed under his weight, more eager for his cock with every second that passed. By the time he shifted to press his hard length against me, I was desperate, wild with need.

He pushed his way inside my slick pussy, taking my mouth with his as he moved in long, slow thrusts. Dylan was taking his time, but I came in a blinding flash, helpless to resist the way he stretched my aroused flesh, the way he ground into my clit when he went deep.

Dylan let me break our kiss to cry out my pleasure. When I was done gasping and moaning, he took my mouth again. Echoes of the orgasm began to build back up as he continued to move inside me in the same deliberate pace.

No one had ever kissed me the way Dylan did. I felt every emotion through his mouth—passion, possession, need, and affection. All of it swirled through me, drawing me into him. The second orgasm was almost on me when he stopped moving and broke our kiss.

I opened my eyes to see him glaring down at me, his eyes clear and bright in the light from the living room.

"No one touches you but me. Never again."

I blinked up at him, resisting the urge to thrust myself on his cock, still buried inside me.

"I should have been there," he said.

"You were."

"Not soon enough," he growled.

"I'm okay," I assured him. "It won't happen again."

"No. It won't." Simple words, but they felt like a vow.

"Dylan." I reached one hand up to his face and rubbed the furrows between his eyes. "It's okay." He jerked his face away from my hand.

"You don't understand. You're mine. Mine. No one touches you. No one hurts you. No one scares you. No one. Not ever."

I didn't know what to say. He was right, I didn't understand. In less than two days he'd gone from propositioning me for the weekend to declaring ownership of me. How had this happened? If he meant it, if this was real…

He must have seen the uncertainty flickering in my eyes.

"Say it," he rasped out, his voice guttural. "Now. Say it."

Meeting his intense green eyes, I whispered, "Yours. I'm yours."

"Mine," he said again and thrust hard into my pussy. "Mine."

Taking my wrists into one hand, he hauled them over my head and pinned me to the bed, fucking me hard, his deliberate, gentle touch transformed into an aggressive claiming. Under the force of his body taking mine, the base of his cock grinding into my clit, my nipples scraping his chest, my brain scattered.

I could think about what this meant later. All I cared about at that moment was Dylan. His heat, his passion, and his need for me. He was all I'd ever dreamed of in a man.

No, he was more perfect than my dreams. He was everything. The blistering heat of my second orgasm took me under. I wrapped my arms and legs around Dylan's body, digging my nails into his back and rocking up, my pussy squeezing him as tightly as my arms. I heard him groan, felt him stiffen as he emptied himself inside me. Then I passed out.

CHAPTER TWENTY-FOUR

LEIGHA

I opened my eyes to a dark room, momentarily forgetting where I was. I shifted to sit up, and the arm tightening on my waist brought me back to reality. I was in Dylan's penthouse.

We'd crashed after the most intense sex I'd ever had. And I thought Dylan had said some profound things in the middle of it. About me belonging to him. Not weekend fling kind of stuff.

Just as I wondered why I was awake, I heard a ping from the side of the bed. My phone. Someone was texting me. Glancing at the clock, I saw it was after two in the morning. Who would be texting me?

Belatedly, I remembered the weird messages I'd gotten earlier. I'd thought they were a mistake, until I saw my name. It had been stupid to hope they'd go away if I ignored them.

I'd just wanted one night of a fairy tale with Dylan. A night when nothing could go wrong. Peter had almost ruined that, but punching him had been a fantasy for a while, so his offensive behavior turned out to be a blessing.

Easing out from under Dylan's arm, I left the bed, grabbing my phone from the bedside table on the way to the bathroom. Maybe it was just one of my friends drunk texting me from a bar. It *was* Friday night. That didn't happen often, but it did happen. I checked the display on the phone. It was not a friend.

I'm tired of all this bullshit.

Meet me at your house at 3am.

The last text had just come in. Tired of trying to ignore this, since the texter was obviously not going away, I typed back,

Who are you? How do you know where I live?

A pause. I held my breath, terrified by the possible answers. Was it someone I worked with?

You know who this is, stupid bitch. Your 10,000 wasn't enough. I want the rest.

Steven. I'd thought he was long gone. My lawyer had looked for him and found no traces of the Steven I'd known. And what did he mean by *the rest*? He'd taken my entire savings account. There wasn't any more to give.

I don't have anything else. You took everything.

I know you have more. I've been through your files. Meet me in 30m or I send this everywhere. Come alone!!!

A second later another text popped up. No words, just a video. Dread pooling in my stomach, I hit play. At the first frame, bile rose in my throat.

It was us, Dylan and me, in the hallway the night before. His hand up my skirt, me clinging to his shoulders, my head tipped back, clearly in the middle of orgasm. Both our faces were easy to see, despite the low light in the hallway. If this got out, there would be no hiding from it.

I sank to the floor of the bathroom, my heart sick with despair. I'd had one night with Dylan. And it had been perfect. He'd been perfect. I'd spent half the time wondering if I really could be falling in love with a man I'd just met.

Now, here it was. Cinderella was turning back into a pumpkin earlier than expected.

A hot tear dripped down my cheek. I didn't want to leave. I wanted to stay, to wake Dylan up and ask him to fix this like he'd fixed that horrible dinner the night before. Like he'd fixed Peter. He would if I asked. Somehow, he could make this problem go away too.

But could he do it faster than Steven could send that video out to news station, blogs, to anyone who'd love to use it to bring one of the rich and famous low? Maybe not.

And this could ruin Dylan. It might not hurt the casino. A secret tryst in a hallway probably played well for the reputation of a guy who ran a casino. But I'd learned that afternoon that the casino was only a small part of his responsibilities.

Dylan ran Kane Enterprises with his brother and a cousin. They were involved in all sorts of businesses and had government contracts with some of them. They also had a board of directors Dylan had described as 'a bunch of uptight old geezers'.

What would those geezers do if Dylan was caught in a sex scandal? Could they push him out? It was possible, depending on how the stock was divided. I couldn't afford to ask, not now.

I knew Dylan would help me. At what danger to himself? Given how he reacted when Peter had manhandled me, Dylan might be pissed enough to go after Peter without covering his own ass.

I couldn't let that happen. Dylan had given me more in the short time I'd known him than any other man. No one else had even come close. I wasn't going to let Steven hurt him. Steven was my mistake. I would make him go away. My phone pinged again.

You have 27m. Then I release the video.

My finger hovered over the phone, blurry through the tears in my eyes. I didn't want to leave. But I had to protect Dylan. Hand shaking, I typed,

I'll be there.

CHAPTER TWENTY-FIVE

LEIGHA

I *'ll be there.*

The text I'd just sent glared up at me like an accusation. I was out of time to debate right vs. wrong. I'd set things in motion. Now I had to act.

It was two thirty-seven in the morning. I had until three am to get to my house or Steven would send out the video he'd taken of Dylan and me in the hallway at the Delecta, Dylan's hand up my dress in the act of making me come, complete with my ecstatic moans.

My stomach rolled at the thought of that video on phones and computers across the world. I wouldn't attract that kind of attention on my own, but Dylan would. He was Dylan Kane.

Plenty of people would love to see such a successful, attractive man brought low. More important, his board of directors would not be happy. If this spun out of control, he could lose the business he'd worked so hard for.

I stood, peeling myself off the cold bathroom floor, and looked in the mirror. My eyes were red, my skin pale, and my hair a dark tangle still caught in the pins from my formal up-do. Frantic, I yanked at the pins, and pulled a brush through my hair.

I had to get out of here without being noticed. Severe bedhead was not going to help. No makeup and a ponytail were a start. The gleam of gold at my throat caught my eye. I'd forgotten the jewelry Dylan had bought me.

I couldn't take it with me. My eyes closed in despair, I unfastened the necklace and removed the earrings, setting them on the counter beside the sink. The bracelet was a little trickier, especially with my sight blurred by tears.

I shut off the bathroom light and cracked the door open. Dylan slept on his stomach, head turned to the side, away from the bathroom and closet. Trying to keep absolutely silent, I crept across the carpet and sneaked into the closet. The drawers holding my underwear opened on smooth bearings, making no sound.

I pulled a pair of jeans from a hanger and hoped they fit. They did. With a dressy blouse, I'd fit in with the casino crowd. I didn't have my purse or my wallet. Ditto on house keys. My phone, with its payment app for some of the local taxis, would get me home. The hidden key beneath my back deck would get me in. That would have to be good enough.

I needed to know how much time I had left, but I wasn't foolish enough to turn on my phone in the dark room. It was going to be enough of a challenge to get out without Dylan hearing. I felt for a pair of shoes on the closet floor, hoping I grabbed something I could walk in.

Still in my bare feet, I sneaked out of the bedroom, every nerve alert for the sound of Dylan moving. All I heard were his quiet breaths.

My heart hurt at what I was doing. He'd hate me for this. I knew it. But I wouldn't let Steven ruin him. Steven had done enough to me. I couldn't allow his ugliness to take anything away from Dylan. As hard as Dylan worked, and as much as he loved his company, he didn't deserve to have Steven jeopardize it all.

At the door to the penthouse, I paused. Dylan used a pass-card to access the penthouse floor. Would I need it to leave? I guessed I'd find out soon enough. The heavy front door was too well built to creak, but I was careful with the handle, afraid it would click into place loudly enough to wake Dylan.

I waited until I was in the elevator, moving to the first floor without needing the key, before I put on my shoes. I'd grabbed high heeled sandals. Not the best match for my jeans and blouse, but they'd do.

Security wasn't watching me as far as I knew. I wasn't a prisoner at the Delecta despite Dylan commandeering my keys and purse. But he might pull up the security cameras to see where I went when I left. I thought about catching a cab from a different casino, but Dylan had my driver's license. He wouldn't have to work very hard to find me. And I was running out of time to meet Steven.

I made my way to the front doors and pulled up the app on my phone to pay for the taxi. Fortunately, one of the taxis that accepted electronic payments was waiting for a passenger. I slid into the back and gave him my address, checking the time. Seven minutes.

I'm on my way, I typed. A few seconds later my phone pinged with a reply.

I said not to be late. My head was twisted with fear and my heart heavy at the decision I'd made. But now that I was committed to leaving, anger was taking the front seat. I'd moved as quickly as I could.

Why did Steven have to be such an asshole about it?

Hadn't he taken enough from me? Now he was getting ready to take more and he couldn't give me an extra five minutes.

I reminded myself that losing my temper would not help. Steven had that video of Dylan and me. He was probably looking for an excuse to use it. Pissing him off wouldn't help me.

The whole point of leaving Dylan was to protect him from Steven. If I couldn't control myself, not only would I be losing Dylan, Dylan might lose his company.

Taking a deep breath to calm my racing heart, I tapped out another text.

Sorry. I had to sneak out. Couldn't rush. Just a few more minutes.

No response. Watching the city flash by outside the window of the cab, I tried to take Steven's silence as a good sign. My eyes blurred as tears filled them.

I didn't want to feel sorry for myself, but I was having a hard time not adding self-pity to all the other emotions roiling inside me. I'd sworn to stay away from men. Then I'd met Dylan, and for once it seemed like I'd found a good man, one worth loving. Now I had to leave him to protect him from my previous terrible choice.

My future stretched before me, clouded by Steven. If he was back for more this time, what was to say he wouldn't return over and over? Especially now that he had that video.

I had no real way to get it from him. I could demand the phone he'd used to film it, but surely he'd already uploaded it to a cloud storage site or put in on a computer. I could never be sure all copies of it were truly gone. Never. It would always exist.

A tiny voice in my head whispered that Dylan could take care of this. He could make one call to Axel and the two of them would be all over it. Except if I didn't face Steven in about two minutes, the video would be out there for the world to see and all the data recovery in the world couldn't stop it.

Steven was an asshole, but he was smart. Maybe if he'd given me a little more time to think this over, I could have come up with a better solution than giving in to blackmail. Twenty minutes had left me barely enough time to dress and flee the Delecta. Not even. Twenty minutes had just passed, and I was still a mile from my house.

Two minutes, I typed.

I'm on your back deck.

Great. The last place I wanted to be with Steven was alone in the dark. But we'd do this outside. I wasn't letting that bastard in my house.

The cab pulled onto my quiet residential street, lined with small bungalows like my own, all dark for the night. I lived in a community of families and older residents. No one would be up at this hour. I couldn't decide if that was good or bad.

Exiting the taxi, I closed the door as quietly as I could and headed around the side of my house. My back deck came into view, enveloped in shadows. I couldn't see Steven, but that didn't mean he wasn't there, watching me.

I kept the spare key to the house in a hidden compartment under my deck, secured by a combination lock. I'd never had to use it before. I hoped the lock still worked.

I waited a few seconds for Steven to show himself. When he didn't, I decided to get the key. I'd have to move it later if Steven saw where I kept it. But I'd worry about that tomorrow. I had enough to stress over without adding about my spare key.

The combination lock was stiff, and I had to lay on my

back in the gravel beneath the low deck, but I got the key. I was coming to my feet, shoving the key in my pocket, when Steven stepped out from behind a nearby tree.

I jumped in surprise, the heels of my sandals slipping in the gravel, but I managed to stay quiet. I really didn't want to wake the neighbors.

The family on the left side of the house had two young kids. They were sweet. On my right was Mrs. Carmody. She had ears like a hawk and hated noise. I was quiet, so it wasn't usually a problem, but if she caught us skulking in the dark on my back deck, she'd call the police. That would be a problem.

"You're alone," Steven said, sounding oddly curious.

"What do you want?" I was surprised at how steady my voice was. Inside I was trembling with fear and rage.

"I wasn't sure you'd be smart enough to ditch the guy. You almost hit the mother-load there, didn't you? How'd you like my video? Hot, right? I must have jerked off watching you come five times already."

"What do you want?" I hissed again, my stomach turning at the thought of Steven watching me with Dylan.

How had I ever thought I liked him? Looking at Steven in the shadows of my deck, he was completely unassuming. By all rights he should have looked like a dirty, greasy weasel.

Instead he was blandly handsome. Blond hair in a conservative cut. Khakis. A dark blue polo shirt. An evil bastard wearing the costume of a normal, everyday guy, and I'd fallen for it.

"You don't want to talk about my movie making skills? How about we talk about distribution? I can have that video up where the whole world can see it anytime. Won't take me more than a minute or two."

"What. Do. You. Want?" I demanded one more time. If he wouldn't tell me what he wanted, I couldn't give it to him and make him leave me alone.

"I want your 401k," he said. "I saw the statement in your files. You've got almost sixty grand in that thing. Sign it over to me and I'll give you the video. And I don't want you to see that guy again. Dylan Kane is a problem I don't need. You go back to him, I show the video."

CHAPTER TWENTY-SIX

LEIGHA

I stared at him in shock. What an idiot. He was right; I did have a lot in my 401k. I was an accountant. I was responsible with money. And Haywood & Cross had a very generous employer matching policy. But I couldn't just withdraw the money and hand it over to Steven.

"That's not how it works," I whispered. "It's not a bank account. I can't go to an ATM or write you a check. I have to fill out paperwork, send it in through my human resources manager. It takes at least a week, probably more. And then there's an early withdrawal penalty. At least 10%."

Steven's eyes narrowed. He kicked one foot at the corner of my deck like a frustrated child.

"You're lying," he said.

"Why would I lie about this? I want that video. I want you to go away."

"You have to give me something. I'm not giving you the video for nothing. Anyway, you make good money and you never spend any of it. I'm not leaving with nothing."

My mind raced furiously. I didn't have anything to give him. No jewelry worth pawning. Same for electronics. He'd already taken my easily accessible savings. Then a thought occurred to me.

"Why the hurry? You know I called the police after you emptied my savings. Did you know I hired a lawyer to sue you?" He shrugged and looked away. "So why risk coming after me? And you obviously know who Dylan is. If I'd told him, he would have crushed you."

"Not before I uploaded that video," Steven sneered at me.

"True, but can you imagine what Dylan would have done to you? So why come after me again? Why not find some other sucker?"

In my panic, the weirdness of Steven's actions hadn't penetrated. I'd only thought of protecting Dylan by coming here to meet him, not why Steven would be doing all this in the first place. Steven shuffled his feet in the gravel and murmured something I didn't catch.

"What?"

"I said, I owe some people money."

"How much money?" I asked. I didn't have cash, but I needed to know how deep in the hole he was. And how desperate he would get.

"Forty grand," he whispered. "These aren't people you owe money to. If I don't get them something by tomorrow, they're going hurt me."

I bit back a scathing comment about how I hoped they broke both his legs. I did, but telling him that wouldn't get rid of him.

"Forty grand? What did you do? Borrow it?"

"No," he whined. "I took your ten grand to a game and

lost it. They gave me a marker for the forty. I was on a hot streak. I was going to win it back, and then some."

"Idiot," I said under my breath. I should have kept my mouth shut. Steven's fist slammed into my face, catching me on my jaw, and sending me to my ass in the gravel.

I'd never been hit like that in my life. His hands weren't that big, but his fist felt like a sledgehammer, the pain ballooning out from my jaw, clouding my head. Saying it hurt didn't really cover it. How did boxers do it? One punch and I was down, stunned and a little confused.

Lifting my hand to my face, I looked at him smirking down at me. How long had he been thinking about hitting me? The knowing smile on his face spoke of a well loved thought made real.

My stomach tightened. Coming here had been a mistake. I should have woken Dylan. I should *not* have tried to deal with this on my own.

"Don't call me an idiot," he said, not looking the least bit sorry about hitting me. "My luck turned. It wasn't my fault."

"I don't have forty grand, Steven. I don't even have twenty."

"You better come up with something, you stupid bitch. I saw you go shopping with that guy. Don't tell me he didn't buy you stuff I can pawn."

"He did," I said in a low voice, trying to soothe him despite my bad news. "But it's all at his place. You could maybe get a few hundred for these shoes."

I pulled at the silver straps, getting the sandals off as fast as I could. I knew they were designer, but I didn't know which one. Used, they could be worth a hundred or a thousand. Steven wouldn't know the difference. Getting to my feet, I handed him the sandals.

"Shoes? That's the best you can do?"

My mind raced, searching for something, anything I could come up with to make him leave.

"My car," I said. "It's only three years old. Paid off. I have the title inside. I'll sign it over to you. It has to be worth at least twenty grand."

I loved that car. A beige sedan, it wasn't exciting on the outside, but I'd splurged and gotten upgrades on the interior. Leather, sunroof, nav system, all the bells and whistles. I'd planned to drive it for at least another six or seven years.

Along with the house, it was the first adult possession I'd purchased after I got my job. But if giving it to Steven would get him to leave, I'd do it. Steven's expression brightened at my offer. His head lifted, and he looked around.

"You came here in a cab. Where's the car?"

"At the Delecta, in the parking garage. The parking ticket is in the driver's side visor. I have a spare key and the title inside. I'll give them to you, and you can go get the car, take it, and sell it first thing in the morning for cash."

"I won't get twenty grand for it if I sell it to a used car dealer," he said, sulking like a child. He might be acting immature, but he wasn't entirely stupid. No way would he get twenty grand for it from a dealer. And he didn't have the time to sell it to a private owner.

"No. But that's the best I have for you. You know I don't have any expensive jewelry or a big TV. That car is the only thing I own that you can turn into cash by tomorrow."

Steven studied the ground between his feet, thinking. My heart thudded in my chest. If I gave him my car, I'd be screwed.

Thanks to his raid on my savings account, I didn't have enough for a down payment on a new one. But that was the least of my problems at the moment. I needed to make

Steven happy enough to leave me alone. And to forget about using that video. Finally, he looked up.

"Let's go inside and get the key and the title."

Relief and dismay swamped me. Relief that he'd take the car. Dismay at being alone in the house with him. I didn't trust him. He'd hit me already. And his admission about jerking off to the video creeped me out. Who knew what he'd do when we were alone?

"I'm not going in the house with you," I said. I wasn't budging on that. Out here I had Mrs. Carmody next door. She was sleeping, but if I screamed, she'd be on the phone with the cops in a second.

Once I was inside the house, all bets were off. "You go in. The title is in my file cabinet, top drawer. In the file labeled Honda Accord EX-L. The spare key is in the same file. You can take them and go."

Steven eyed me warily. "You're not going to ask me for the video?"

I rolled my eyes. "Is the only copy on that phone?" I asked. Steven scoffed at me.

"Of course not."

"Then what's the point of getting the phone from you? You could have a hundred copies of the video stashed all over the place. But you know what would happen if you used them, right? The only thing keeping me from calling Dylan is that I don't want that video to get out. If you release it, he'll come straight for you. You do know that, don't you?"

Steven glared at me, his jaw clenched tight. He knew I was right. A single woman with few resources was a good target for his brand of petty blackmail.

But if he drew Dylan's attention, he was fucked. Once

that video was released, Dylan would have no reason to hold back. And I had nothing left for Steven to take.

"I want your 401k," Steven said. I shook my head. He didn't know when to give up.

"Steven, you don't have time for that. It'll leave a huge paper trail. And Dylan will want to know why I ran out on him. He's going to come find me."

As I said that, I realized it was the truth. Dylan would be pissed. He might hate me and want nothing more to do with me. But he'd at least track me down to get an explanation.

My heart sank. If I told him the truth, he'd go after Steven. And as twitchy as Steven was, he might release the video the second he caught sight of Dylan. He could have already uploaded it to streaming sites, just one click shy of going wide. I needed to convince Steven to get out of Vegas.

"You need to take my car, trade it for cash and get lost. Find the rest of the money you need somewhere else. Like New York. Or Miami."

"I told you to stay away from Kane," he said. "You go near him, I'll release the video."

"I'm not going back to him, okay? But he knows where I live. He may come here. I can't control Dylan Kane. This is your only chance. Take my car, get as much cash for it as you can, and run like hell. Don't bother coming back for more. This is it. I don't have anything else to give you. It'll take me years to make up for what you've already taken."

"Fine. But I'm not leaving you alone out here. Open the door and get in the house."

CHAPTER TWENTY-SEVEN

LEIGHA

I wasn't expecting Steven to move so quickly. Before I could dodge him, he was behind me, one hand over my mouth, the other trapping my wrists.

Steven wasn't a big guy, or a powerful one. He didn't need to be; he was stronger than me. He shuffled me up the two steps to the deck and toward the sliding door of my kitchen.

"Open it," he ordered.

I yanked on my right wrist. I couldn't unlock the door without a hand free. At that moment, I wished I'd invested in some self-defense classes. Steven had me immobilized, and I had no idea how to get away.

If I'd been wearing my heels, I would have had some kind of weapon, but in bare feet all I could do was kick his shin. He let go of one wrist and I fished the key out of my back pocket. The door slid open, letting out a puff of cool air.

Pushing me toward the table, Steven hooked one foot

around a chair and pulled it out. He let go of my mouth and wrist to shove me down in the chair.

I scrambled to get my feet under me. His fist caught my already bruised jaw in a flash of pain, sending me back down into the seat. A drawer opened behind me and I heard the rasp of duct tape being peeled off the roll. That seemed to be my luck tonight.

Steven hadn't done a single dish or cooked one meal in that kitchen. But he'd taped up a tear on his favorite tattered sneakers, and apparently he remembered where I kept my duct tape.

No more men, I told myself. It would take me years to forget how badly I'd fucked up my life by picking Steven. He taped my wrists together behind me, then wrapped the tape around my torso over and over so I couldn't get up. When he was sure I was secure, he left me, disappearing down the hall off my kitchen.

It didn't take him long to find the title to my car and the spare key. I was organized and everything was exactly where I'd told him it was, the file folder complete with a neatly printed label courtesy of my handy little label printer.

When this was over, I was going to try being irresponsible. No more savings, no more 401k. Fuck my tidy filing cabinet. What had all that gotten me? Heart broken and victimized by a two-bit con artist. Tears pushed at the backs of my eyes. I fought them back. I wasn't going to cry in front of Steven.

He held out the title and my urge to weep vanished. I'd have to sign the title over for him to sell the car.

In Nevada a transfer between private citizens required a bill of sale and a title, but no notary. I'd looked into it for an elderly client who'd been newly widowed and had never sold a car before.

I'd let Steven worry about the bill of sale, but he had to know I'd have to sign the title. Not easy to do with my hands duct taped behind my back.

I didn't need to say anything. Looking from me to the title, he realized his mistake. Again displaying his maturity, he slammed the paper on the table and kicked the leg of my chair.

What an ass. It wasn't the chair's fault he was an idiot. I had a moment of triumph before my brain kicked in and reminded me that I was currently taped to a chair in my kitchen and about to sign my car over to this moron. So who was the stupid one? Steven wasn't a genius, but neither was I.

Cursing under his breath, Steven yanked open drawers until he found one with a knife. Then he did the same looking for a pen.

When he had both, he slashed at the tape on my wrists, freeing them with one slice that cut the side of my wrist along with the tape. I felt a cold burn, then blood began to well on the side of my free wrist. He cursed again. Yanking the title away, he snarled,

"Don't bleed on it."

"Then get me something to wrap this up," I snapped. "It's not my fault. I didn't cut myself."

More evidence that I wasn't as smart as I thought I was. Mouthing off to an angry guy with a knife was not the best idea. He grabbed a dishtowel, wrapped it around my bleeding wrist, and taped it in place. It hurt like a bitch, worse than my jaw.

It wasn't bleeding fast enough to be dangerous, but it was bleeding more than I'd like. Quickly, before blood could soak through the towel and stain the title to the car, I scanned the document and signed it over to Steven.

The second the pen left the paper, he snatched the title away from me, folded it up and shoved it into his back pocket. Tossing the knife in the sink, he wrenched my arms behind my back and taped them together for the second time. Standing back, he examined me before saying,

"You look good like that. Tied up and helpless. Makes your tits look bigger. I always liked your tits. They made up for your fat ass."

A sharp bolt of fear hit my heart. No, not this. He could have the money, he could have anything. I didn't think I could take it if he touched me.

Steven grinned at the terror in my eyes. I flinched back, trying to get as far from him as I could. Taped to the chair, I couldn't move very far.

One hand reached out to stroke my bruised cheek. I jerked my face away, looking down at my lap, shamed by the tears leaking from my eyes. He laughed, dropping his hand to cup my left breast. I'd managed to put on a bra in the dark, but it was thin. No barrier from the harsh squeeze of Steven's hand. Desperate, I said,

"Touch me one more time and I'll scream so loud Mrs. Carmody will be on the phone with the cops in a second."

His hand fell away. Steven knew Mrs. Carmody. She'd come out on her front porch and yelled at him more than once when he'd parked his car too close to her yard.

"That old bitch," he murmured. "I could just do this." He ripped off a length of tape from the roll and held it out, moving toward my face. If he gagged me, I couldn't do anything.

I opened my mouth to scream, and he punched me

again, this time on the cheekbone. My jaw snapped together. Tape slapped across my mouth, sealing it shut.

I panted through my nose, heart racing. If he tried anything else, I was going to fight. Forget about the knife, forget about the fucking video.

Steven could take the car, but he wasn't taking anything else from me. Maybe he sensed my resolve. After staring in my eyes for a long second, he shrugged.

"You're not worth the trouble. Not for a fat chick." He turned for the back door and said over his shoulder, "You'll get yourself loose eventually. Don't even think about calling Kane or anyone else."

I didn't respond, just stared at my knees and waited for him to leave. He hesitated, as if thinking of saying something else, then he was gone, sliding the glass door to the deck closed behind him.

I sat there, taped to the chair, fighting tears. I wanted to let go, to sob out my frustration. Crying wasn't going to help me. My wrist was bleeding, and I was pretty sure it needed stitches. Since I didn't have a car, I'd have to call a cab to take me to the ER.

At least I had my health insurance, though the ER co-pay was going to cost way more than an office visit. But I didn't think this could wait until Monday.

Before I could get to the hospital, I had to get out of this chair. Wiggling back and forth, I eased the chair back toward my kitchen cabinets. One thing at a time. First, I had to get my wrists free, then get a cab to the hospital. After that, I could worry about the rest of my life.

CHAPTER TWENTY-EIGHT

DYLAN

I rolled over and stretched, my arm extended for Leigha. I'd been dreaming of her. Of taking her from behind at the end of the bed while she wore nothing more than those gold heels. I reached out my hand and met cold sheets. My eyes flashed open, and I scanned the bed. No Leigha.

Sitting up, I looked to the bathroom. Dark and empty, the door hanging open. Aside from the startled rasp of my own breath, the penthouse was silent. It felt empty.

Swearing under my breath, I leaned over and flicked on the light beside the bed and checked the clock. Three seventeen am. Getting out of bed, I took a quick walk through the rooms of the penthouse. Nothing. But then, I already knew. I felt her absence in the quiet, cool air. Leigha was gone.

I was not an emotional guy. In business and in my personal life, I was all about logic. At the realization that Leigha had walked out on me, logic went out the window. Anger hit me first.

What the fuck was wrong with this girl? Had she seen

an old lipstick in the bottom of a drawer and decided I was hiding a secret wife? Was I not good enough for her? I was Dylan fucking Kane for fucks sake. Women panted to get in my bed and this one little accountant, who lived in a bungalow and drove a beige sedan, thought she could walk out on me? Fuck that. Fuck her.

I paced my bedroom in a fury, dragging on discarded clothes as I went. I may have knocked over a lamp in the process. I know I threw our champagne glasses at the fireplace.

Not my most mature moment. Fumbling with a button down shirt I'd worn that afternoon, I caught a whiff of her perfume. This was the shirt she'd been wearing while we'd eaten lunch. While we'd talked all afternoon.

That girl wouldn't have walked out on me without a word. She'd gotten nervous that morning, but everything had changed between us. Hadn't it?

Taking a steadying breath, I went to the second bedroom and opened the hidden storage closet in the back corner of the room. Her suitcase was still there, her purse and car keys sitting right on top.

I could see her walking out on me. No, I couldn't. But I could accept that it had possibly happened. But even if she'd decided to sneak out in the middle of the night, what woman would take off without her purse? Or her house keys?

Something here wasn't right. Forcing myself to stop and think, I ran through the options in my mind.

Then I went to my desk. Opening my laptop, I picked up the phone and dialed the number of the security office. As I listened to the phone ring, I clicked on my email and pulled up the preliminary report Axel had sent me on Leigha.

I'd had him look into her, that Steven guy, and her new boss. The report was nothing in depth, Axel hadn't had time for that. But it had the basics: home address, social, license plate as well as make and model on her car, and employment history. It was a start. On the other end of the line, I heard, "Delecta Security, this is Randall."

"Randall, it's Dylan. I have a situation. I'm on my way down, but I want you to get started right away. I need footage of anyone leaving the penthouse floor after midnight tonight. And I need you to locate a vehicle in our garage. A Honda Accord EX-L, beige, Nevada plate NGT947. If the car isn't in the garage, find footage of it leaving the garage. And last, have someone check the entrance for an individual getting picked up or getting into a taxi. I'm sending a picture to your email."

"Yes, sir. I'm on it. Anything else?"

"No. I'll be right there."

If she'd left the casino, I'd know in minutes. And if she was still here, I'd have my security team pick her up and deliver her to my office.

For a second I wondered if she'd sneaked off to gamble downstairs. As soon as the image hit my mind, I laughed. Not Leigha. I couldn't imagine Leigha gambling her hard earned money for fun, much less sneaking out of my bed to do it. She was my good girl. And as my head cleared, worry made a tight ball in my chest.

She *was* my good girl. If she was going to leave me, she'd at least tell me goodbye. She wouldn't disappear in the night like this unless something was wrong.

I was dressed in the jeans and button down I'd been wearing earlier in the day, but I needed shoes. Flicking on the light to the bedroom, I noticed that everything was in place.

Her jewelry was still on the bathroom counter, her dress neatly hung up in the closet. There were two empty hangers among the clothes Melissa had bought her. Probably jeans and a shirt. If she'd taken a dress, only one hanger would be empty.

Pins littered the sink. And her phone was missing. The last I'd seen it, she's left it on the bedside table. Now it was nowhere to be seen. Had someone called her?

Shoving my feet in a pair of worn sneakers, I grabbed my wallet and keys before heading for the door. I was going to find her. And when I did, she'd have some serious explaining to do. I was worried, but I was still pissed off.

I tried her cell in the elevator and got her voicemail. I thought about hanging up, but decided not to. Instead, I waited for the tone and said, "Leigha. I woke up, and you weren't here. Call me."

Calm and thoughtful. Nothing that would piss her off if she'd decided she was mad at me. I didn't like that she wasn't answering her phone.

CHAPTER TWENTY-NINE

DYLAN

The security room was hopping when I got there. It usually was on a Friday night, no matter that it was past three o'clock in the morning. I ignored the bank of screens in the front and went straight for the back office.

Up a half-flight of stairs, the office was sealed off with glass and overlooked the rest of the security nerve center. Randall glanced up from the screen in front of him when I opened the door. He'd been with me since I opened the Delecta. With thirty years in the business and a kid's enthusiasm for the newest tech equipment, he was the ideal head of security.

Every potential card cheat or scam artist was a new puzzle for him to solve. I knew he'd track Leigha down at warp speed if just for the rush of answering the question of what she was up to.

"I got her, sir," he said. I sat beside him and studied his monitor. Divided into four sections, he had Leigha on one, frozen in the act of pressing the button for the casino floor inside the elevator.

The second frame showed her outside the door to the casino, getting into a taxi. The third was scanning cars in the garage. I glanced to my left and saw one of Randall's top techs examining the cars on his own monitor. The fourth frame showed vehicles exiting the parking garage.

"She got in the cab at two twenty eight. Went straight down to the lobby and outside. Didn't stop or talk to anyone on the way. Nothing in her hands but a cell phone. Not even a purse. Here, I'll show you."

Randall clicked open another screen on the monitor and clicked a tab. The cameras tracked Leigha from the moment of pressing the elevator button, through her ride to the lobby.

A different camera picked her up as she left the elevator, the frames changing quickly now as she moved from camera to camera on her path to the exit.

The last shot showed her carrying only her phone, getting into a cab. Through it all, her face was blank, her jaw set. She looked pale and shaken. If I'd doubted it before, now I was certain. Something was very wrong.

"Find the car," I said to Randall. "If it's still here, keep eyes on it, just in case."

Standing up, I pulled out my phone and paced to the far corner of the room, dialing Axel. Everyone would hear my conversation, but these guys were smart enough to pretend not to listen. I didn't have time to go to my office for privacy, I needed to be here until I got another lead.

"Hey," I said when he answered with a clipped, "What?"

"Leigha is missing. She left without her purse or keys and caught a cab about an hour ago. Something's wrong."

"You're sure?"

"Yeah. I'm sure. Do you have a guy you can send to her house? If she's not there, you need to track her down. Her car is still here, so are the rest of her things. I don't want to go running all over town looking for her if she's planning on coming back."

"One minute." He hung up.

Axel was fast. Fewer than two minutes later, my phone was ringing again.

"I've got a guy headed to her house and another listening to the police band for any mention of her car. I sent a third to the Delecta. He'll be on hand if you need anyone there. What do you want my guy to do if she's at home?"

"Have him make sure she's okay. If she's fine, just let me know and I'll head out. If she's in any trouble, he should do whatever he has to."

"On it. Stay there and as soon as I have anything, I'll call."

I hung up and went to stand behind the tech monitoring the garage. Cars flashed by on the screen, too fast for me to identify.

"How will you know if you find it?" I asked, trying to distract myself. I'd feel more solid once I knew where Leigha was. Without looking up at me, the tech said,

"We built it off the facial recognition program. I entered the vehicle specs we had on file for the car, and the computer does the rest."

"You have the specs for all those cars on file?" I asked.

"No." The tech shook his head without taking his eyes from the screen. "But we have just enough to cut the time it takes to scan the garage. Too much data to parse would slow it down."

"You guys build this in-house?"

"Yes, sir. More secure that way."

"Very cool," I said, studying the cars speeding across the screen. I'd invested a lot into my security team. Between the high rollers visiting the Delecta and the amount of cash that came in and out, it was imperative to have the best watching over the place.

I rolled my shoulders back, trying to relax. I had my team here watching for her. Axel was on the case. We would find her. And I'd either solve her problem, whatever it was, or spank her ass for trying to run out on me again. Likely both.

Sometime in the last day and a half, I'd decided I was keeping Leigha. She was everything I'd been looking for in a woman, and I didn't see the point in playing games.

I'd always been like this.

Decisive.

Once I knew what I wanted, I never questioned it. I'd met Axel in college and in the time it took to get through our first Biology Lab, I'd known we'd be friends for life.

When I'd decided to move to Nevada and open a casino, I'd spent over a year gathering intel and researching the market. But once I'd come out to find a building site, I'd chosen it the first day.

One look at the aging casino in the Delecta's current location, and I'd known this was the place. I could see it in my mind, cleared of the original building, my beautiful Delecta rising in its place. I'd made an aggressive offer on the property, done my due diligence and made a solid investment.

But all that was to keep the spreadsheets looking good. I'd already known I'd found my new home.

I barely knew Leigha. What I did know left me wanting

more. Beautiful. Un-fucking-believable in bed. Smart. Sweet. Funny. Just touching her calmed me and set me on fire at the same time.

I had no idea why she'd left. Maybe I was wrong, and she wasn't in trouble. Maybe she'd gotten another wild idea and decided she had to go. If that was it, I'd change her mind.

I was Dylan-fucking-Kane. I could get her back. Thinking over the possibilities, I hoped that was it. The other option, that she was in trouble, was too terrifying to contemplate. At least, it would be terrifying until I got her back. Once she was safely with me, I was going to unleash holy hell on whoever had upset her.

"Sir, we've got the car." I turned to see Randall and the tech leaning over the tech's monitor. It was stopped on her sedan, the license plate clearly in view.

"Keep an eye on it," I ordered. "It's possible she may come back to pick it up."

"Yes, sir."

We waited, all three of us watching Leigha's car, sitting alone and untouched in the quiet parking garage. Until Axel called with a report from Leigha's house, or she showed back up in the casino, there was nothing I could do.

I was all about action. Sitting and waiting while Leigha might be in trouble was not my idea of fun.

It felt like an eternity of nothing, the same view on the screen of Leigha's boring, brown car. I was buying her a new one. That one wasn't her.

She thought she was a sensible beige sedan, but after the way she'd looked that evening, I think it was safe to say Leigha was a rare bloom. She needed something exciting, not sensible. An Audi TT.

I pulled up the website on my phone while I waited. In

the middle of choosing between silver and grey, Randall said,

"We've got movement."

Jerking my head up, I saw a blond male approach the car with a single key in his hand. I heard Randall say,

"Track him back to where he entered the Delecta." Somewhere off to the left a voice answered, "Yes, sir."

"Do you know him?" Randall asked, zooming in on the man's face. I didn't. I called Axel, who picked up immediately.

"I've got a guy getting in Leigha's car. He had a key. Does your guy at the Delecta have the make and model?"

"Yes. Hold on."

I heard Axel pick up another phone and relay orders to his man outside the casino. Before he came back on the line, there was a beep on his end, then the sound of a muffled voice. Our call was muted on his end for less than a minute, then Axel was back.

"My guy at Leigha's house checked in. She was there, just left to get in a cab. He's in his car following the cab."

"Where's she going?" I asked.

"We're not sure yet," Axel said, "He's on her. But Dylan, there's something else."

"What," I barked, not liking the hesitant tone of Axel's voice.

"My guy was there with a partner. When they saw Leigha leaving, he stayed with her and the partner checked the house. The back door was unlocked, and he went in.

There was a bloody knife on an armchair by the door and blood on the kitchen table and floor. Duct tape was stuck to a chair. The best he can tell, she was injured and restrained. Hard to say what came first. Our best guess is that her cab is headed to the hospital."

Mind numb, I hung up the phone and shoved it in my pocket. Turning to Randall, I said, "Email a screenshot of the man in Leigha's car to Axel. I'm headed out. If anything comes up, call."

I saw the doubt in Randall's eyes. He wanted to stop me from leaving. If I looked half as frantic as I felt, he had good reason for his concern. I didn't care, the only thing on my mind was Leigha.

Injured and restrained. The words echoed in my head. Who would hurt Leigha? Why? I paced through the security room, headed for the elevator when the door opened. Axel stood there, his phone to his ear. Reaching out, he grabbed my arm and pulled me into the elevator.

"I'm driving," he said, "You look like shit."

I scowled at him, but said nothing, my entire being focused on getting to Leigha.

CHAPTER THIRTY

LEIGHA

The shot of local anesthetic for the stitches didn't hurt that badly, but seeing the needle poke through the open cut on my wrist was revolting. I knew I shouldn't have watched. I tried not to.

It was like passing an accident on the freeway. You mean to look away, but at the last second, your eyes swerve to the ravaged car, dreading to see the destruction and unable to stop yourself.

Aside from my wrist, my jaw was bruised, the skin hot and tight with swelling. The ER nurse had given me an ice pack for it. It helped, but I was getting tired of holding it in place.

And it looked like I was going to have at least six stitches when this was over. Strike that, seven. Or more. Steven's careless slash of the knife had done more damage than I thought.

Working my way across the kitchen while taped to a chair hadn't helped. Neither had getting the tape loose enough to free my wrists. I'd maneuvered myself to the side of the kitchen cabinets where a former owner had screwed in a set of metal hooks for dishtowels.

They didn't do much to tear through the duct tape, but I was able to catch one of the hooks under the edge of the tape and pull on it, dragging it down my arm to my wrist where it was looser.

It sounds easy after the fact, but at the time, bleeding and freaked out, it felt like it took forever. Every tug on the hook had moved the tape a fraction of an inch and pulled at the open wound on the side of my wrist.

Steven's knife alone probably hadn't cut me that much. By the time my wrists were free, I'd done more damage than he did.

Once I got the tape loose, it hadn't been that hard to get my uninjured arm free. Painful, since it involved more yanking against my bleeding wrist, but not difficult.

Cutting the tape around my torso was easy enough once I had my hands back. I hadn't bothered to unwrap and check my arm. I'd grabbed my phone, called a cab and wrapped another towel around it.

Waiting for the cab had been terrifying. I was sure Steven had left. He was an asshole, but not a complete idiot. He would have gone straight for my car in case I had second thoughts. But what if he hadn't? What if he was going to come back?

I'd huddled in an armchair by my front window, hidden from the street by thin curtains, gripping the bloody knife from the sink in my good hand. If Steven did come back, I'd be prepared.

When the cab finally showed, I dropped the knife, threw a jacket over my arm so the cab driver wouldn't see the blood, and ran out the front door, not bothering to lock it behind me.

The hospital was having a slow night - my only bit of good luck so far. Even without my ID or insurance card, it wasn't long before I was sitting behind a curtain, wearing a hospital gown over my jeans, and watching the doctor in green scrubs sew up my arm.

Another bonus; he was a plastic surgeon they'd called down and I wouldn't have much of a scar. Even a day as bad as this one had a few minor bright sides. They hadn't given me anything for the pain, aside from the local anesthetic for the stitches, but I felt drugged.

Maybe it was the adrenaline crash. I didn't know. Now that I was safe in the hospital, I couldn't seem to get it together.

My thoughts spun in sluggish circles. What if Steven came back? What if he decided to release the video anyway? What if he told the guys he owed money that I was responsible for it and they came after me?

Hadn't I seen that in some movie? The guy gets in debt with the mob and he tells them his brother is responsible for him so they went after the brother? Or maybe that was because the brother vouched for him? No, it wasn't his brother; it was his best friend. Wasn't it?

I stared at the lights on the ceiling, trying to make sense of what was happening. Exhaustion dragged at me, slowing my mind and weakening my body.

I had to figure out what to do. I had no car, no wallet, and I didn't want to go back to my house. It didn't feel safe anymore. Not since Steven had been there, touching my things and taping me to my own kitchen chair, his hand on my breast, his eyes ugly and angry. I couldn't go back there. Not tonight.

They'd asked if I had someone who could come get me. I'd said I did. I guess it wasn't a lie. I could call my mother.

Somehow I'd convince her not to take me back to the Delecta. I couldn't go there either. Ever.

If Steven caught me anywhere near Dylan, he'd release the video and all this would have been for nothing. Tears pricked at my eyes.

I gritted my teeth and sucked in a breath through my nose. No crying. Not here, where everyone could see. Later, when I'd figured out what to do and where to go. I'd cry later.

A scuffle at the curtain caught my attention. I heard an aggravated voice say, "Sir! You can't just -" The curtain was thrown back.

Dylan stood there, glaring at me, his friend Axel just behind him. Relief at seeing him flooded through me. Dylan was safe. Dylan wouldn't hurt me. Then I remembered the video. Dylan couldn't be anywhere near me.

I wanted to jump up and demand he leave, to scream that he had to go. I didn't move. For one thing, the doctor was still stitching up my arm. And for another, I was frozen in shock. How had he known where I was?

The nurse looked my way and said, "He insisted on seeing you. Do you want me to call security?" I shook my head. Dylan didn't speak either, his eyes flipping between me and the doctor working on my arm.

A minute later, the doctor tied off the last stitch and wrapped my arm in a protective bandage. Standing, he patted my shoulder.

"Someone will be in to discharge you and give you instructions on caring for the stitches. You were lucky." Glancing over his shoulder at Dylan and Axel, he whispered, "You're safe here. Are you sure you don't want to make a police report?"

His eyes grazed over the bruises on my face. I hadn't

offered much of an explanation of what happened. I shook my head again.

"No. They didn't hurt me. I promise. I'm safe with them."

"You're sure?"

"I'm sure. I swear."

"Okay. I'll get a nurse in to discharge you." He stood, patted my shoulder once more, and left, sending a suspicious glare at Dylan and Axel as he went.

When we were alone, I said, "You have to go. You can't be near me."

Dylan ignored me, striding across the room to take my face in his hand. His body vibrated with fury, but his touch on my bruised cheek was gentle.

"What the fuck happened to you?" He asked, his voice quiet, but hard. "Who fucking did this to you?"

"Dylan, I mean it. You have to go. Please. Just go. I can't help you if you won't go." I heard my voice rising in hysteria. He couldn't be here. All of this was for nothing if Steven found out we were together and released the video. "You have to go. Please, Dylan, just go. Please."

He didn't go. Instead, he sat beside me on the hospital bed and pulled me into his arms, pressing my unbruised cheek into his shoulder. I didn't struggle. I should have.

I should have jumped off the bed and run to get away from him. But he was so strong, and he smelled comfortingly familiar, warm and clean and male. Somewhere deep in my head, I knew I was panicked and irrational.

Steven wasn't at the hospital. He couldn't be watching me. But logic wasn't getting through at that moment. I was scared, in pain, and only just registering how much worse things could have been with Steven.

Flashes of the bloody knife and the way he'd touched

me played across the insides of my closed eyelids. I felt myself begin to tremble. I tried to stop it, but it was as if my body was no longer under my own control.

Shaking, tears warm on my cheeks, I burrowed into Dylan. I'd always thought I was a strong woman. Most of the time I was. With everything that had happened that night, my inner strength had deserted me.

"Can you tell me what happened?" he asked in a low, soothing voice. "Why do I need to leave you?"

I drew in a ragged breath. I needed to tell him. He needed to know why it was dangerous to be near me.

"Steven took a video of us." Another ragged, tear filled breath. "In the hall. The other night. It's -" I cut off, unable to go on. I'd brought this down on Dylan. Me. It was my fault this was happening. "You can see everything."

"Okay," he said, voice still gentle. "We can deal with that. That doesn't explain your face. And your arm."

He rubbed his hand up and down my back as if I was a child woken from a nightmare.

"He said if I didn't meet him at my house he'd release it everywhere. It's bad. You can see our faces. I was afraid -" I stopped and dragged in a breath. "Your board. Stockholders. It was bad, Dylan."

I felt him sigh against me. His hand on my back continued its rhythmic, soothing strokes. The worst out in the open, I relaxed into him. Now he knew. Everything he'd worked for was at risk because of me. Fresh tears spilled over my cheeks. I was so tired. Cold, aching, and tired.

"Why didn't you wake me? Why did you just leave, sweetheart?"

"Not enough time," I whispered. "He said I had to meet him at my house in twenty minutes or he'd send the video out. There wasn't enough time. And he said if I saw you again, he'd send it out."

Footsteps sounded beside the bed. "The ex," Axel said in a low voice. "He took off with her car."

"It was Steven?" Dylan asked, tucking a stray hair behind my ear. "He's the one who did this to you?"

"You can't go after him, Dylan. He'll use the video. Please."

"I can take care of the video, Leigha."

I forced myself to pull out of his embrace and sit up. Meeting his eyes was harder. When he'd come in, he'd been glaring. Now his eyes were soft. Concerned. Not angry.

"What if you can't? What if he sends it out to YouTube and all the other sites. You'll never be able to get it back. And your company - the board. They could -"

He cut me off with a finger to my lips. Before I could think of something else to say, he looked over his shoulder at Axel, who was talking into his phone in a clear violation of hospital's no cell phone policy.

Seeing the grave expression on his face, I didn't think Axel cared about hospital policy. Gone was the serious but relaxed guy I'd met earlier that evening. This man was all deadly focus as he gave quiet orders into the phone and hung up. His eyes met Dylan's in a promise.

"I'm on it," he said.

"You heard all that?"

Axel nodded. "We'll pick him up. Get the car back. Don't worry about the video. I'm out. I'll have your people send a car."

He disappeared to the other side of the curtain. Dylan reached for me, and I leaned back.

"Dylan, this is too dangerous. What if -"

"Do you trust me?" he asked, eyes on mine.

I wanted to look away. I couldn't. It felt like he was asking for more than just trust, like he was asking me for everything. I couldn't lie to him. I was scared. For him. For myself. My head spun, I hurt all over, and I desperately wanted to lie down and sleep.

I'm not sure I could have lied to him under normal circumstances. But sitting on that hospital bed, exhausted and my emotions a mess, I was helpless to resist the force of his will.

"Do you trust me?" he repeated.

I told him the truth.

"I do."

"That's all I needed to hear."

Dylan pulled me into his chest and resumed his gentle strokes on my back. I must have drifted to sleep, because the next thing I knew, a nurse came in and Dylan was gently sitting me up so she could give me my discharge papers. She said something about my not having my insurance.

Dylan pulled a card out of his pocket and handed it to her, saying, "Have billing call my office on Monday, we'll take care of it."

The next thing I knew, he was carrying me, over the nurse's protests, out of the hospital and to the black car waiting outside. I zoned out again on the way back to the Delecta.

I didn't realize I'd fallen asleep until I opened my eyes to see Dylan's soft sheets as he lowered me into his bed. A moment later, he joined me, pulling my body into his until my head rested on his shoulder, my injured arm on top of his chest.

The last thing I felt before I passed out completely was the thump of Dylan's heart beneath my ear, strong and reassuring.

CHAPTER THIRTY-ONE

DYLAN

I t was all I could do to keep from hunting down that bastard myself. The look in Leigha's eyes when she'd seen me - relief, then terror. It tore at me. She'd done this for me. To keep me safe. Had it even occurred to her that if that video got out she'd lose her job?

I wasn't in the tabloids every week, but I had my share of attention. If the video got out, it would be huge news. Overnight, Leigha would become a sex tape star. Completely unemployable and good for little more than hosting a third rate reality tv show. Or other options far worse.

I could answer that question. She hadn't thought of herself at all. She'd been completely out of it at the hospital, pale, close to shock, and scared. In no condition to play a game with me.

She could have accused me of putting her in that situation in the first place. She never would have been in that hallway, exposed to prying eyes with my hand up her dress, if I hadn't dragged her along. I didn't think that had even occurred to her.

It meant something to me that she'd been looking out for me. Something big. And it said a lot about her. But fuck, he'd hurt her. Terrified her.

I was taking her in to press charges in the morning. I planned to hold her hand through all of it though I'd have to watch myself. I had a feeling there was worse she was hiding than a bruise to the jaw and a knife wound.

At least the bruises were contained to her face. I'd undressed her unconscious body for bed, my stomach tight with the fear that I'd find matching bruises on her body, her breasts and her thighs.

If I had, I might have left her and gone with Axel's men to bring Steven in. Then I might have killed him.

It's always hard to say what we might or might not do in an extreme situation. Laying in bed, Leigha's perfume drifting up from her hair, her warm body pressed into mine, I hoped I'd be smart enough not to do anything crazy, like kill a man in cold blood. Even *my* lawyers couldn't get me out of something like that.

At the thought that he might have hurt her worse than he already had, that he could have raped her - the ice in my gut told me there was no limit to what I would do to keep her safe.

Still, she'd earned herself some punishment. I'd go gentle, since her face and her wrist would still hurt when she woke up. But Leigha needed to learn about trust. She'd said she trusted me in the hospital. She probably thought she meant it.

More likely, she *wanted* to mean it. I needed it to be deeper than that. I needed her to trust me all the way. To her soul. And the best way to show her what that meant was with a good, old-fashioned spanking.

Sometimes the cliché was true. Actions did speak louder than words. In the morning, Leigha would find out for herself.

CHAPTER THIRTY-TWO

LEIGHA

I woke up draped across Dylan's chest, his hand stroking my hair. I felt surprisingly good, considering the bruises on my face and the stitches in my wrist. Turning my head, I came eye to eye with Dylan's phone. He wasn't just awake; apparently he'd already been busy getting things done.

"How are you feeling?" he asked, meeting my eyes.

"Okay." I shifted to sit up and leaned into the pillows beside him, laying half on my side so I could see his face. He looked concerned, sweet, and determined. The determined part gave me a shiver. I couldn't tell if it was aimed at me or someone else. Maybe both.

"I'll order up breakfast in a little while. Does your wrist hurt?"

"It's not too bad." It wasn't. It throbbed, but not as much as I would have expected considering I had seven stitches.

Dylan reached towards his bedside table and handed me two brown pills and a glass of water.

"Ibuprofen," he said. "Take them now before you start to move around too much."

I did, staring at the light yellow stretchy bandage the doctor had wrapped around the dressing he'd put on my arm. It would look terrible with my dress for the wedding. The bruises on my face would be even worse.

At the thought of Christie's wedding, my stomach sank. The last thing I wanted to deal with was my sister's wedding.

"What?" Dylan asked, catching my expression.

"The wedding. I feel better, but I don't feel up to going to Christie's wedding. And I really don't want to face questions about this." I raised my bandaged wrist in the air.

"If you want to blow it off, I'm all for it."

"I can't," I said, wishing I could. But my mom would be both furious and disappointed. I could handle the furious part, but I didn't want to disappoint her.

"I know," Dylan said. "Don't worry about the arm. Lola is sending over elbow length gloves. They'll be a little too formal, but better than anyone seeing your wrist. And I had Melissa schedule someone to come up to do your hair and makeup this afternoon. They'll cover the bruises so no one will know anything happened."

"Did you do all that while I was sleeping?"

"You were out cold. Never even flinched when the phone rang."

"Oh." I could be a deep sleeper, but not usually that deep. Must have been a stress hangover from the night before. "Have you talked to Axel? Did he stop the video?"

"It's fine."

"And?"

"And, it's under control," he said, that determined look

taking precedence in his eyes. I guess it was directed at me after all.

"I need to know more than that. What did he do?"

"Do you trust me?" Dylan asked. I remembered him asking that last night at the hospital. I'd said I did. Now that I was awake, the question seemed to have more depth.

At the time I'd been overwhelmed with fear, pain, and relief at seeing Dylan. After a night of sleep, I wasn't sure I'd give the same answer. Did I trust him?

"I do," I said. "But I want to know what's going on."

"And I'll tell you. First, I want to talk about trust."

I stared at him, not sure what to say. I'd said I trusted him. What more did he want?

"Last night," he went on, "That bastard called and threatened you. What did you do?"

"Dylan," I whispered, wanting to stop him.

"You ran," he said, ignoring my protest. He'd been so focused on taking care of me, I hadn't realized he was angry.

"Dylan," I said again, trying to explain. Dylan was done with explanations.

"You ran away," he repeated. "Tell me what you should have done, Leigha. What should you have done when he texted you?"

"There wasn't time."

"Tell me," he insisted, sliding out of the bed so he could pace out his frustration. "What should you have done when he texted you?"

I looked down at the sheets, avoiding his angry eyes and the distracting sight of his naked body. He was so pissed he didn't seem to care that he was naked, but I didn't think this was the best time to be ogling him.

"I should have woken you up," I muttered, feeling like a recalcitrant child.

"Yes. You should have woken me up and trusted me to help you."

His patient, firm tone suddenly struck a nerve. I was an adult, and I'd made the best decision I could at the time. He didn't have the right to tell me what to do.

"I was trying to help you," I said, irritated. I didn't want to go over all this. I wanted to move on.

"I appreciate that, Leigha. I do." He reached out and took my chin in his hand, lifting my face so I was forced to meet his eyes. "It means a lot that you thought about me first. But do you have any idea what went through my head when I realized you were gone?"

"I'm sorry," I said, finally seeing it from his point of view.

"I was more pissed than worried until I saw you get in that cab. You didn't look like you were mad at me, you looked scared."

I had been. I'd been terrified.

"Then Axel called to say they found blood in your house. That you'd been tied up. I love that you're the kind of woman who thinks of others first, but you need to be more careful. What happened was bad enough, but it could have been so much worse."

At that I looked up, remembering Steven's hand on my breast, the way he'd held the knife. Dylan must have seen something in my face.

"What did he do to you?" Dylan demanded. I sat up straighter, tired of cowering away. Dylan was pissed, but he wouldn't hurt me.

"Nothing I haven't already told you about," I said, meeting his eyes. "I promise. He only touched my breast over my shirt and threatened me. That was all."

Dylan swore and spun on his heel, swinging out at the

lamp on the bedside table. It flew across the room and hit the wall, the metal fame gouging a chunk out of the drywall before it fell to the carpet.

"I'm going to fucking kill him," he said, his eyes fierce.

"Dylan, stop." I rose to my knees in the bed, clutching the sheet around me. "Calm down."

"No," he said, turning to point a long finger at me. "My job is to keep you safe. He could have raped you. Killed you. And I wasn't there to protect you."

"No, Dylan!" I yelled, trying to break into his rage, "I was trying to protect you. Don't you understand? I'm okay. This isn't that big a deal."

He stopped and looked at me, his eyes suddenly calm. Coming closer, he sat on the edge of the bed and took my hand. His abrupt change in mood unnerved me.

"This is the biggest deal, Leigha. He cut you. He drew your blood, scared you, and stole from you. He threatened to rape you. While you were with me. And you didn't trust me enough to let me keep you safe. You thought you had to risk yourself to protect me."

"You don't understand -"

"No, Leigha, it's you who doesn't understand. We have something here between us. Something important, but you don't seem to get it."

"What is it that I don't understand?" I asked carefully, looking from his intent green eyes to my hand in his. His fingers closed tightly around mine.

"That you're mine. You belong to me."

"What?" My voice hit my ears in a shrill tone. What did he mean, I was his? This was just supposed to be for a weekend. And despite any evidence to the contrary, like the shopping trip or Dylan showing up at the hospital, I was still afraid to hope for more.

"You're mine, Leigha," he repeated. "I know it scares the shit out of you, but that doesn't change anything."

"I'm not scared," I insisted, lying through my teeth. I was terrified.

"I know you're scared," Dylan said, his eyes patient. "Because the other option is that you don't want me and I know that isn't true."

"Cocky," I whispered under my breath, calculating the odds of making it to the bathroom and locking the door behind me before he could stop me. Not good. It's not that I wanted to get away from him. I just needed a second of privacy to clear my head. Dylan Kane was an overwhelming man.

"Not cocky, sweetheart. I know you want me. Not because of me, because of you."

I didn't speak, only looked up at him. Maybe it was shock, or lack of sleep, but I was having a hard time following the conversation. Dylan went on, with the same patient expression.

"When was the last time you went to bed with a man you'd just met?"

I stared at him, my mouth open. Once. When I was in college. Not needing my answer, he kept talking.

"Yet you did it with me. Not an hour after we met, I had my fingers inside you. Two hours later I was fucking you. Ever done that with another man?"

I shook my head, my cheeks flaming pink. When he put it like that, I sounded so cheap.

"I -" I shut my mouth, not sure what I'd been about to say.

"Do you want to tell me why, Leigha?"

Dylan brought my hand to his mouth and kissed my fingers. A hot tingle shot through me, straight to my pussy.

How could I be this confused, this annoyed, and still get turned on? It was the mystery of Dylan Kane.

In response to his question, I shook my head. Any answer I could think of would leave me too vulnerable. Because the real answer wasn't an answer at all. Why had I done all those things with Dylan when I'd barely known him?

I'd done them because in some way, I felt like I'd always known him. Like we fit together. He set things off inside me that I'd never experienced with any other man. Not just the orgasms, although those were life changing on their own.

Dylan pushed me, dared me to take risks. With him, I felt safe outside my normal comfort zones.

Suddenly, everything he was saying made sense. I trusted him. I had from the very first moment. Right up until Steven had stepped in with his video, and everything fell apart.

"It's alright," he said, leaning in to kiss my lips. "I know why. I know why you ran, and I know why you came back. So do you. But now, I'm going to prove it to you."

"What?" I breathed, hoping he meant the talking was over and it was time for sex. Dylan reached up and tugged away the sheet covering my naked body. His eyes raked me from my bare breasts to the dark vee of hair between my legs and back up to my face.

He grinned, that determined glint back in his eyes. A thrill of fear and anticipation ran down my spine.

"It's time for your punishment, Leigha. It's time for me to show you what trust really means."

CHAPTER THIRTY-THREE

LEIGHA

He stood and reached out his hand for mine. I took it, nervous about what he had planned, but not ready to say no. I knew in my heart that if I stayed where I was our relationship would be over. Whatever was coming, it was important to Dylan. Too important for me to back away, not if I really wanted something with him.

I followed him into the living room where he sat on the couch, his posture oddly formal. I stopped, not sure what I was supposed to do. Dylan gestured to his lap.

"Face down, over my knees."

Realization washed through me. He couldn't be serious.

"You're going to spank me?" I asked, incredulous. I knew people did this, and Dylan was definitely bossy in bed. But spanking me was a little weird.

"Yes," he said, the devilish glint in his eyes sending heat through my uncertain body. "And you're going to like it."

"I don't think so," I said, eyeing his lap. Dylan grinned again, that same knowing, determined grin that got me wet.

"You will," he said. "This is it, Leigha. This is trust. I'm asking you to do something you think you'll hate. You need to trust that I'd never hurt you. Trust that I'll take care of you."

"And if I can't?" I asked, my voice thin.

"You can."

I closed my eyes for a long moment, imagining what would happen if I turned and walked from the room. Despite his determination, and his declarations that I was his, somewhere inside myself I was certain this was a deal breaker for Dylan.

He wanted my trust. If I wanted him, I was going to have to try. I didn't want to live my life afraid of loss.

Maybe Dylan would break my heart if I gave it to him. But there was a chance he wouldn't. All he was asking, this magnificent, brilliant, beautiful man, was for me to give him a chance to prove that he was worthy of my trust. When I thought about it that way, how could I say no?

I opened my eyes to see him, patient and silent, waiting for me. Too nervous to be slow, now that my mind was made up, I crossed the living room and lay across his lap, face down.

He reached to position my injured arm safely along my side. My face burned with embarrassment and I was glad he couldn't see.

I was getting more comfortable with my body, but not enough to feel good about presenting myself to Dylan ass first. My rear end wasn't exactly my slimmest attribute. Before I could go too far down that train of thought, he distracted me with a sharp smack to the body part in question.

I gasped in a breath. *It hurt.* Not as bad as a knife to the arm and getting stitches, but it didn't feel good. The second smack, on the other side of my ass, was just as bad. I blinked my eyes against the welling tears.

Why did he want this from me? He'd said he wasn't going to hurt me, and this fucking hurt. The third smack, just where my ass met the top of my thighs, stung like the first two.

"Dylan," I sobbed. Before I could go on, he smoothed a hand over my smarting flesh.

"Shhh. I know it stings. It always stings at first. This is where you have to trust me. You're made for this. I can tell." He stopped his gentle strokes and smacked me again, three times in rapid succession. The pain built with each stroke until my rear end was glowing with it.

It took all my will to stay still over his knees while tears trickled from my eyes. I opened my mouth to protest, then shut it. He'd asked for trust.

By the next set of smacks, I was gritting my teeth. Dylan was determined to do this, and I was equally determined not to complain. With everything he gave me, if he got something out of spanking me, I could learn to deal with it.

At least, I hoped I could. But I really didn't get it. Taking a break, he smoothed his hand over my ass again.

"You're so red, sweetheart. You're going to feel this for the rest of the day. Probably into tomorrow. You're almost there."

Almost where? Almost done? I sighed in relief. I was ready to be finished with this. I braced for the next hit, prepared to weather the pain.

It never came. The smack did, striking the fullest part of my ass with restrained power. It should have hurt. I guess it did, in a way.

All I really felt was heat. A weird, prickling heat that was frighteningly close to pleasure. What the hell?

The next smack was more intense. Harder. I shifted into it, the strike of his hand bringing more of that new sensation. How did this feel good? He was still spanking me. Harder than before.

I squirmed, brushing my nipples against the fabric of the couch. They were beaded tight with arousal. My body was spinning out of my control.

At the next smack, I arched my back, raising my ass to his hand. It fell, sending hot flares of pleasure everywhere it touched. When I felt the brush of his fingers between my legs, I gasped, this time in shock at how wet I was. When had that happened? One long finger pushed inside and I thrust back onto it.

"Do you want me to stop?" he asked, his voice low.

"No," I moaned, wiggling to get more of his finger. My whole body throbbed for more. More of the spanking, more of his finger. More of everything.

"At least a few more of these," he said, withdrawing his finger and laying another smack on my rear end.

This time, I rocked up into it, asking for it with every inch of my body. I took the next one the same way. And the next. My head was in the clouds, drifting in hot, dreamy, pain-sharpened pleasure, wanting only more of whatever he would to give me.

This was it. This was what Dylan meant by trust. And I'd almost walked away from it. The last smack was harder than the rest, a flare of pain and pleasure so acute, it drove me to the edge of orgasm. Writhing over his legs, I heard myself moaning and gasping. He stroked his hand over my red ass with reverent care.

"I think a little more and you'll come for me," he said. I quivered under his soothing touch. I would. I knew I would. "Maybe next time we'll try that. I bet if I clamped these luscious nipples and spanked you, you'd come so fast your head would be spinning."

I shivered, knowing he was right. I would. I was close as it was, teetering on the edge of release, my body both wound tight and floating in space. Feeling myself move, I realized Dylan was turning me, lifting me into his arms.

He carried me through the penthouse and a few seconds later he lay me down in the bed, positioning my bandaged arm out to the side.

The soft sheets were cool on my heated backside, a momentary distraction before his body came over mine, his hard cock pressing into me in a long, slow thrust that stretched me open.

Just minutes ago, I'd wanted to run from the way Dylan overwhelmed me. Now it was everything, his body over me, his cock inside me. Everything I could touch, hear, smell, was all Dylan.

I raised my legs around his hips, clamping my thighs tight, rocking up into him. If he'd gone a little faster, I would have come right away.

As it was, I didn't last more than a few minutes, driving my fingernails into his shoulders as I came. Dylan kept going in the same steady pace, his mouth on mine as pleasure rose again.

Each time my hips rolled down, the tender, pink skin on my ass burned. Dylan's sheets couldn't have been any softer, but my ass was too tender from the spanking. The sparks of pain made the pleasure sharper, more acute.

The second orgasm grew slowly, the stretch of Dylan's cock inside me a fraction better each time he filled me, until I was again on the edge of coming.

This time, he was with me. Tearing his mouth from

mine, he called out my name as he came, his pounding cock taking me along with him.

Before I could get my bearings, he was up, disappearing into the bathroom. He came out a few seconds later holding a wet washcloth. Careful of my arm, Dylan grabbed my legs and slid me to the side of the bed, spreading my legs wide. He couldn't possibly be ready again. I could barely move.

The warm, damp cloth pressed between my legs, stroking my still sensitive flesh. I tried to slam my legs closed, the intimacy too much. I already felt vulnerable. Dylan blocked me with his body.

Before I could form a verbal protest, he was done. Tossing the washcloth back onto the bathroom floor, he picked me up and set me on my feet.

"Breakfast should be waiting for us. Do you want a robe?" His green eyes twinkled at the question. Did he think I was going to say no? Maybe I'd eat breakfast naked one of these days, but not today.

"Please." He settled a thin, white, french terry robe around my shoulders. I wondered what else I had hanging in that closet. I hoped I'd have time to explore it later. Maybe when I found out what 'later' would bring.

CHAPTER THIRTY-FOUR

LEIGHA

A wheeled room service cart waited just outside the front door of the penthouse. Dylan rolled it in to the table where we'd eaten the day before. I took a seat, the smell of coffee and food reminding me I was hungry.

Dylan put the covered plates, cups, and coffee on the table, then pushed away the cart. Before I realized what he was up to, he'd picked me up out of my seat, sat down in his own, and arranged me in his lap.

"This is better," he said into my ear. I squirmed on his lap, feeling weird about sitting there to eat. Wasn't I too heavy? Putting a voice to my thoughts, I said,

"I'll crush your legs. I can sit in my own seat." His arm tightened around my waist.

"No fucking way. You feel perfect, and you can eat right here."

Hmmph. I made a rude sound in my throat but gave up on sitting in the other seat when he lifted a bite of omelet to my mouth. Ham, cheddar cheese, and rich, creamy eggs.

Yum. The other plate had French toast with home fries. Double yum.

I let Dylan feed me for a few minutes, unasked questions simmering in my mind. I was learning that I was more likely to get what I wanted if I let Dylan have his way, at least at first. Besides, I was starving.

The eggs were mostly gone when I finally put up my hand to stop a loaded fork. "I'm full, for now. I want some coffee and I want to talk about the video."

Dylan put the fork back on the plate and poured me a cup of coffee, adding a splash of cream, exactly the way I liked it. He didn't say anything until I had the cup to my lips and was taking the first sip.

"Axel got the video. His guy followed Steven from the Delecta to his hotel and grabbed him. Axel and his team went through everything. It's wiped it from every source."

"Did Steven send it out?" I asked. I guessed the answer was no since Dylan was so calm. But I'd feel better if I heard it straight out.

"No. He had it backed up on a cloud server, but he left tracks everywhere. Axel followed his steps personally and verified the video was gone. They took his laptop and his phone and scared the shit out of him."

"And then?" I asked. I'd only seen Axel twice, but his foreboding expression at the hospital was enough for me to know I never wanted Axel to try to scare the shit out of me.

"Then they let him go," Dylan said, suddenly not meeting my eyes. He covered by pulling the French toast closer and cutting it into bite sized pieces with the side of his fork.

"They let him go?" I asked, putting down my coffee. "Why didn't Axel have him arrested? Because they had to break into his hotel room and then destroyed evidence?"

Dylan cleared his throat. "Not exactly. I think you should go in and press charges later today. But when Axel found out who Steven owed money, he decided he'd let things play out instead of calling the cops."

"I don't understand," I said. The night before I'd been in shock. Not physically, but mentally. My only focus had been on stopping Steven from sending out that video. I hadn't exactly been evaluating the finer points of the situation.

Now that I was safe from Steven and the video was erased, my brain was kicking into gear. If I hadn't had the threat of the video hanging over my head, I would have reported Steven to the police. So why hadn't Axel done that as soon as he'd made sure the video wouldn't go out? Dylan's answer wasn't reassuring.

"He hurt you, Leigha. He deserves to pay. Axel saw you in the hospital. We think the same way and he didn't even have to ask me. When Steven admitted he owed Sergey Tsepov money, Axel decided to let Tsepov handle the justice part."

"Who is Sergey Tsepov? What will he do to Steven?" I asked. I wasn't sure I wanted to know the answer.

"Russian mob," Dylan said, shortly, still not meeting my eyes. "And I don't know what Tsepov will do to him. Nothing good."

"Dylan-" I cut myself off. I wasn't sure what to say.

"What?" he asked, finally looking at me, his eyes blazing. "The police would throw Steven in jail and maybe he'd do some time. After seeing you getting sewn back together, Axel assumed I wouldn't want to wait that long for payback. He was right."

"But-"

"But what, Leigha? Are you trying to protect him?"

"No." Everything in me revolted at the idea of protecting Steven. "No, I'm not."

"Then what?" Dylan asked, his eyes searching my face.

"I don't know," I said. I didn't. It's not like Dylan had sent this Russian guy after Steven. Owing money to the Russian mob was Steven's mistake. Axel and Dylan just hadn't gotten him out of it by turning him in to the police. Still... "Will they kill him?"

Dylan shrugged, looking unconcerned. "I doubt it. But I'm not in on the specifics of how the Russian mob handles delinquent loans." He must have seen the doubt in my face, because he went on, "Axel wouldn't have let them have him if he thought they'd kill him, sweetheart."

"So Steven's with the mob?" I asked. I had a hard time picturing it. I didn't know anything about the mob, Russian or otherwise, but I couldn't imagine Steven, average, normal looking Steven, a prisoner of the mob. "What happened?" Dylan sighed.

"You're not going to let go of this until you know everything, are you? You can't just trust that I've got it under control?"

"Are you serious?"

Dylan raised an eyebrow at me in answer.

"I trust you. As far as I can trust anyone I've only known a few days, I do trust you. But this is my life. Steven stole from *me*. He attacked *me*. I know you want to make this easy for me, but I need to know what's going on. I'm never going to be the kind of woman who wants to hand over all her problems for someone else to solve. If that's what you want -"

"It's not." We glared at each other. Then Dylan sighed again. "It's not. I know I have a habit of wanting to be in control. You're going to have to deal with that. But I can work on not taking over."

"Fine," I said. "I'll consider it my job to keep you from thinking you can take over the world."

"No. You can consider it your job to figure out a way to put up with me while I take over the world."

"I can figure out how to put up with you trying to take over," I shot back, "Just don't try to shut me out of my own life."

"So I shouldn't tell you what Axel found out about your new boss?" I stiffened in Dylan's lap. I'd forgotten about mentioning my boss's name the first night we'd met.

"Don't do anything to my boss. I like my job."

"Even if you're working for a guy who's had three sexual harassment suits filed against him in the past five years? All dropped, and the women involved aren't talking."

"Why?"

"My guess is money or threats. Maybe both. But I've seen this guy's picture and money seems more likely."

I couldn't say I was surprised. My old boss had been great. He'd had high expectations, and he worked my department hard, but he'd been my first real mentor out of college. His replacement was slimy, way too touchy, and despite that, not threatening enough to get an angry woman to drop a lawsuit.

"What a creep," I said, reaching for my abandoned coffee cup.

"Do you want me to get him fired?" Dylan asked, casually. I choked on my sip of coffee. Could he do that?

"You can't just get him fired!"

"Because you think it's wrong or because you don't think I could do it?"

"Both," I sputtered. "Don't get him fired."

"So you *do* think I could do it," he said, grinning at me.

"I don't want to find out. I can handle this," I said.

"I don't like you working for a man like that."

"Tough," I said, my mind racing. "He hasn't actually done anything inappropriate. If he does, I'll let you know."

"Will you?" he asked. I sank back against him, relaxing into his hard chest, my half full coffee cradled in one hand.

"I will," I said. "I promise. I don't want to be groped at work. If he steps out of line, I'll tell you. But until then, stay out of it."

Dylan grunted in response and stabbed a piece of French toast with his fork. I hoped it was for him because I was stuffed.

I hadn't missed that he'd changed the subject earlier. I still wanted to know what had happened to Steven. After fending off the French toast, I said, "So, are you going to tell me what happened to Steven? How did Axel know the Russian guy caught up with him?"

"You really won't let this go?"

"Nope."

"Fine," Dylan said. "Axel's guy sat on the hotel after they dealt with Steven. About an hour after Axel left, Steven came out, got in your car and drove to an empty parking lot behind a salvage yard. Axel's guy watched to see what was going to happen."

"And?" I asked.

"And two guys who work for Tsepov showed up. Steven tried to give them your car as part of the payment. They beat on him for a while, then took him and your car somewhere."

"So they have my car?" That sucked. I needed my car.

"Don't worry about it," Dylan said. "I'm getting you another one."

"What?" I would have screeched it, but I was laughing at the same time. Dylan was nuts. Even if this was the beginning of a relationship instead of a fling, which I wasn't sure it was, he couldn't go around spending all this money on me. Ignoring both my protest and my giggles, he turned his head to kiss my temple.

"That car wasn't you."

"It was practical. Efficient. I'm practical and efficient."

"You make yourself sound boring," Dylan said. This time, he was the one laughing.

"I am boring."

"Trust me. You're not boring. And you might be practical and efficient, but you're also gorgeous, clever, fun, and unbelievably sexy. Not a woman who should be driving a beige sedan."

"You're insane," I said. He didn't answer. Not in words. Instead, he took the mug of coffee from my hands, set it on the table, and kissed me.

I didn't even try to resist. Since the moment I'd met Dylan, I'd been overwhelmed, confused, and undeniably drawn to him. My analytical brain always wanted an answer for everything, but the rest of me wasn't worried about the details anymore.

I wanted Dylan.

I wanted this; his mouth on mine, and his strong hands pulling me close.

CHAPTER THIRTY-FIVE

LEIGHA

I shifted to face him and kissed him back, burying my hands in his thick hair. We'd had so many different kisses. Rushed kisses. Demanding kisses. Hungry kisses. This kiss was slow. Easy. As if we had all the time in the world.

And maybe we did. I was the one who kept thinking about the expiration date on this arrangement. Was it time to let go and just enjoy what we had?

I moved again, bracing a foot on the floor so I could turn and straddle Dylan. I was tired of worrying about what all of this meant. For once, I was going to relax and enjoy.

I settled onto his lap, my robe parting in the front, exposing my breasts. Dylan's hands found them immediately, his fingers stroking and twisting my nipples, sending sparks of arousal straight between my legs. We'd had sex an hour before, and I was ready again. So was he.

His thick cock rose up, only the thin cotton of his boxers between us. I pushed into him, his groan of pleasure making me even hotter. It gave me a rush knowing that I could do this to him. That Dylan Kane was this hard for me.

Breaking our kiss, he tipped me back, supporting my weight as he dropped his mouth to my breast. Suddenly, at the sucking heat, the tease of his tongue, I was no longer willing to take my time.

I gasped for breath and ground my pussy down onto his hard length. With one hand, I groped for the opening in his boxers. If I could just drag them down a little bit, he'd be mine.

Realizing what I was up to, he grabbed my wrist and tucked my arm gently behind my back, careful of my stitches even in the midst of our rising passion.

"Not yet," he said, his lips moving against my sensitive nipple in a caress. "I've been wondering if you're one of those women who can come from having her nipples sucked. Now I want to find out."

My pussy heated at the thought. I hadn't even known that was possible, but if he thought it was, I was willing to give it a try. Arching my back a little more, I nudged his lips with one nipple.

Dylan gave it a hard, long suck, the pressure transforming into sharp need. I squirmed against him, unable to stay still as he moved from one breast to the other.

"I wish I had clamps for these," Dylan said, pinching both nipples at the same time.

I looked at the hard, deep pink tips caught by his fingers. I'd never worn nipple clamps, but I wished he had some too. If they felt anywhere near as good as his fingers, I'd love them.

The spanking had opened up a whole new world. I'd never imagined pain could bring so much pleasure. Dylan's mouth returned to my breast, his lips drawing hard, his fingers working my other nipple with a squeezing pressure that might have hurt if I hadn't been so turned on.

My nipples had a direct line to my clit, each pinch and suck arrowing between my legs as if Dylan was touching me there and not solely focused on my sensitized breasts. I writhed against him, my empty pussy clenching, desperate for his cock.

It was building, an orgasm unlike any I'd had before. From a distance, I heard my moans rise. The scrape of Dylan's teeth dragged a gasp from my throat.

Beside us, Dylan's phone vibrated and beeped, clattering against the wood. We ignored it, too lost in desire to care that someone was calling. Whispering my name, Dylan switched sides, my wet nipple beading even tighter with cold once the warmth of his mouth was gone.

Again, the phone rang, buzzing and beeping in insistent tones. A niggle of worry penetrated my lust soaked brain. The third time the phone came to life, Dylan leaned back with a curse. Picking up the sleek, black phone, he barked,

"What?" I couldn't hear the voice on the other end, but I sobered immediately as Dylan went still beneath me. He murmured, "You're sure. Okay. Yeah. We're on our way. Thanks. See you there."

Moving with deliberate care, he set the phone down on the table and met my eyes with a weighty gaze.

"Leigha, we have to go." He stood, lifting me gently before setting me on my feet.

"What's wrong? Is it my Mom?" I couldn't imagine what else could have made him shift so quickly from passion to concern. If it had been the video, he would have been angry. There was some anger simmering in his green eyes, but mostly he looked worried.

"No, not your Mom." With one hand on my arm, he

ushered me to the bedroom. "We need to get dressed." I dug in my heels.

"What's going on?"

"Get dressed and I'll tell you in the car."

I thought about arguing, but his careful, quiet manner had me freaked out. Standing in front of the closet, I reached for a sundress. Dylan stopped my hand and pushed the hanger with the dress aside, grabbing a pair of jeans instead. I took them and fished around in my underwear drawer for panties.

By the time I had them on, Dylan had picked out a top for me and was getting dressed himself. I took a minute to brush my hair and refasten it in a pony tail. It was still stiff from all the hair spray I'd used the night before. I needed a shower, but whatever was going on, it didn't look like a shower was on the agenda.

Dylan had his keys in his hand as I exited the bathroom. To my surprise, he also carried my purse. Things must be serious if he was returning my purse. For a second, anxiety chilled my heart.

Was he getting rid of me? No, he was being far too sweet to be dumping me. Maybe he'd gotten my purse from its hiding place because he'd finally realized I wasn't going to leave him. Not unless he tossed me out.

His arm wrapped around my shoulders in a protective embrace as we headed to the elevators. I leaned into him, nerves rising as he remained silent, the serious expression on his face growing more pained with each moment. And more pissed off.

"Will you tell me what's going on now?" I asked, my voice low, as if I could soothe whatever had him upset. He gave me a tight squeeze and shook his head.

"Not yet. I want to tell you in private and we need to get moving. As soon as we're in the car, I'll fill you in."

"But no one is hurt?" I asked. Even though he'd said this wasn't about her, my mom was still on my mind. Something happening to my mom was the only thing I could think of that would be truly awful at this point.

Unless this had to do with the video. Now that a little time had gone by, more of the implications of the video had hit me. My first thought had been for Dylan, but my practical side had emerged to point out that the video would do me far more damage than it could strike at Dylan.

He had the money to rebound if he lost his company. If it got out, I'd absolutely lose my job and no reputable accounting firm would hire me.

"And it's not the video?" I asked in a small voice. He'd assured me it was taken care of, but the unexpected happened every day. Look at me, snuggled up to Dylan Kane. Unexpected was a massive understatement. He wrapped both arms around me, dropping his head to kiss my hair.

"No, it's not the video," he whispered. "Forget about that video. Axel's guys found every copy of it. It's gone. And we'll be careful in the future. I won't let you be exposed like that again. I promise."

The vehemence in his voice was both comforting and alarming. My nerves ratcheted up another notch. I knew better than to ask him what was going on again. If he didn't want to tell me until we got to the car, he wouldn't.

Endless minutes later, buckled into the passenger seat of his Maserati, I waited for him to break the heavy silence. Now that we were alone, he didn't drag it out.

"Your house is on fire. Your neighbor was out watering her flowers an hour ago and saw smoke coming from your kitchen. She called the fire department. They're there now."

"Who called you?" I asked, my thoughts frozen aside from the most basic questions. My house was on fire. How could my house be on fire? I hadn't left any candles burning. The electrical systems weren't new, the bungalow itself was decades old, but I'd had everything checked thoroughly before I'd moved in.

"Axel."

"How did Axel know?" It didn't matter. What mattered was my house. But I couldn't quite get my head around that.

"He put cameras on your door. Part of a security system I asked him to install. They got an alert on the fire around the same time your neighbor saw it. If he'd had a chance to put in the full system, he would have known soon enough to catch it."

"It's bad?"

Dylan turned to look at me, his eyes concerned. "We'll know more when we get there."

CHAPTER THIRTY-SIX

LEIGHA

I was numb. For the rest of the ride I stared out the window, watching the familiar streets of Vegas fly by. My house was on fire. If the fire was big enough, the house would be a total loss.

My house.

Everything I owned was in that house. I had good insurance. Actually, it was great insurance. I wasn't worried about the money. I was broke, but that was what insurance was for in the first place.

I'd be able to repair any damage, even buy a new house if I had to. But I'd never get back the pictures of my Dad, or my high-school debate team trophy, or Bugsy, the stuffed rabbit I'd had since I was in infant. We'd been inseparable until I started kindergarten. He was threadbare and faded, but I still loved him. He was on a bookcase in my bedroom. Maybe he'd be okay.

The warm pressure of Dylan's hand around mine yanked my mind out of its useless wanderings. I wouldn't know how bad it was until we got there. We were only a few minutes away and there was no point in worrying about the damage until I saw it for myself.

Four minutes later, I wished I hadn't seen it. My cute little bungalow was engulfed in flames. They were stronger by the kitchen, but had spread to every part of the structure I could see. Tears blurred my eyes.

Dylan parked the car on the opposite side of the street, three houses down, away from the confusion of fire trucks and flashing lights. He was opening my door a few seconds later.

Axel was on his way to us by the time we were walking toward the house. He met us in the middle of the street, putting out a hand to prevent us from going any further.

"They've blocked the street from the other side," he said, "We can wait here. They'll need to talk to you, Leigha."

"What do you know?" Dylan asked, taking my hand and pulling me close to his side.

I leaned into him, needing his strength. My eyes were riveted to the flames shooting through the roof of my little house. I didn't need to ask, I already knew it was a total loss. My heart squeezed with grief, and my stomach rolled from the acrid scent of my life burning to the ground.

I'd never been particularly materialistic. Maybe it was the accountant in me, always saving money instead of spending it on things I didn't really need. But this wasn't a new sweater or a big TV.

It was my home.

The first I'd ever bought and one I'd expected to have for years to come. It was the first place that was all mine, a haven where I'd felt free to be myself. I'd painted the walls myself, had chosen each pillow and curtain to fit my vision of a cozy refuge. Now it was well on its way to being a pile of ash.

I was so distracted by the fire, I almost missed hearing the word, 'arson'. My head popped up, and my mind came back into focus. Arson? I didn't have to work hard to come up with the one person who might have burned down my house.

"Are you sure?" I asked, interrupting Axel and Dylan's quiet, intense conversation. Axel turned his sharp eyes to me.

"There's an empty gas can in the back yard. The police have it, hopefully he was stupid enough to leave prints. They could smell the gas he spilled on his way in. They'll have to complete their investigation, but that this point they're sure it's arson."

Dark rage welled in my chest. My brain was screaming, 'why?'. It was a stupid question. There was never a 'why' for something like this. Steven was a stupid, greedy asshole, and I'd been naive and blind enough to let him into my life.

My breath came in choppy waves, my lungs tight with emotion and the caustic smoke clouding the air. Dylan turned me into his chest. Over my head, I heard him say,

"We fucked up. We should have taken him in last night."

"Not your call, man. This is on me," Axel responded, his voice heavy with regret.

"No. You knew what I would have said, and you did it. Fuck."

Dylan rubbed a hand over my back, I think soothing himself as much as me. He was right, if Axel had called the police the night before, Steven would probably be in jail right now instead of running free and torching houses.

I didn't have it in me to be pissed at them. Maybe later.

Just then I was too grateful for Dylan's arms around me to be mad at him.

"Any idea how he got away from Tsepov?"

"No. I called a guy I know who's in with Tsepov, but he's not talking. I did get the feeling that Steven will be lucky if the cops pick him up before Tsepov does."

"Do they need her for anything? I need to take her home," Dylan asked.

"No, take her home. I let the lieutenant know she was on her way, but he won't be able to get to her for a while. He can talk to her later. She'll be with you?"

"Yes. Just give him my number and we'll make ourselves available."

"She up for pressing charges about last night? I gave his name as the likely suspect - I told the lieutenant I was working security for her as a client's girlfriend and gave him what we know about Steven - but this will all go faster if she makes a statement herself. They can't hold him on anything related to last night without Leigha," Axel said.

Reminded that they were talking about me, and I could speak for myself, I lifted my head from where I'd burrowed into Dylan's chest and said, "Let's go now, before it gets too late. I have to start getting ready for Christy's wedding in a few hours."

"I think your Mom would understand if you missed the wedding, sweetheart," Dylan said, looking down to meet my eyes.

"I'm not missing the wedding. And I want to press charges against that asshole."

"We're leaving," Dylan said to Axel, turning us to face his car. He kept me tucked into his side as we walked away from the mess of firetrucks. Behind us, Axel called out,

"Leigha!"

I ducked under Dylan's arm and faced Axel. His handsome face was dark with remorse.

"I'm sorry," he said. "I thought I was doing the right thing."

I shrugged, not sure what to say. He hadn't acted out of malice; he'd been looking out for what Dylan would want. It was hard to fault him for trying to be a good friend even though his decision had played a part in Steven setting my house on fire.

Without a good response, I settled for raising my hand in a wave. Axel nodded his head and disappeared back into the smoky crowd of firefighters working to contain the blaze before it could spread to the other houses.

Dylan was opening my door when I heard my name shouted across the street. I turned to see Mrs. Carmody bearing down on me, her teacup terrier, Jimmy, tucked into the crook of her arm.

Short, scrawny, and tanned a deep, nut brown, she vibrated with energy. It wasn't the crisis, Mrs. Carmody was a live wire all the time. If she was awake, she was on the go.

"Where have you been? And who is this?" She narrowed her eyes at Dylan, her gaze as suspicious as if he'd been holding a Molotov cocktail and a match.

"This is Dylan Kane," I said, stepping a few inches away from Dylan. "He's... we're... I've been with him."

Dylan offered Mrs. Carmody his hand. She took it, but barely spared him a glance.

"I thought you were home," she said flatly. "I couldn't get in the back door. I thought you were caught in there until the firefighters told me the house was empty."

She didn't sound concerned, but after a few years of living next door to her, I knew that she was hiding her true feelings. If she'd chased me down in the street, she must have been terribly worried.

Knowing she would hate it, but not sure how else to reassure her, I leaned down and pulled her into a hug. She leaned into me for a single breath. Yep, I'd scared her. Guilt welled even though it wasn't my fault.

"I'm so sorry, Mrs. Carmody. Do you remember Steven? My ex-boyfriend?" She nodded, her eyes shifting harder with dislike. I went on.

"He attacked me last night and stole my car. I had to take a cab to the hospital for this." I lifted my bandaged arm. "Dylan took me home with him and I only just found out about the fire."

"And the one in the suit? Why did he say he was working for you?" Mrs. Carmody gestured toward the firetrucks in front of my house where Axel had disappeared. She had ears like a bat and hated missing out. I wasn't surprised she knew so much of what was going on.

"He works for Dylan in security. He was helping with Steven." Not a great explanation, but I wasn't sure what else to say. Mrs. Carmody sniffed as if smelling something revolting.

"I never liked him. He kept parking with his back tire on my lawn. You think he came back and did this?"

I nodded.

"And what about him?" She gestured to Dylan. "How does he fit into this? I would have noticed that car in your driveway, young lady. Are you spending the night with a man you just met?"

I flushed a fiery hot red. I didn't know how I could let Dylan display me naked in front of the room service waiter and still managed to blush in front of Mrs. Carmody. I looked up at Dylan in helpless embarrassment. He aimed his most charming smile at Mrs. Carmody and stepped in to save me.

"Leigha and I are dating. I would have said you'd be seeing my car in front of her house more often, but given what's happened, I think she'll be staying with me."

"And where do you live?" she asked, studying him with still suspicious eyes. With a straight face, he said,

"I live at the Delecta."

"You're not taking Leigha off to live in a casino. She's a good girl. And she doesn't need to get tied up with another loser who gambles too much."

I giggled. I couldn't help it. Mrs. Carmody met her cronies somewhere on the strip every Wednesday night for a buffet and a night of playing the slots. She spent far more time in casinos than I did.

"I don't gamble, Mrs. Carmody," Dylan told her. She drew in a breath, probably to protest, when I jumped in.

"He lives at the Delecta because he owns it," I said. A light came into her eyes, and I inwardly groaned.

"So you can take care of her?" she asked Dylan, ignoring my second, vocal groan. Dylan, still completely serious, nodded.

"I can. She won't have to worry about anything."

"Good. Make sure she has some fun. The girl works too much, never gets out to have a good time."

I rolled my eyes to the sky, partly embarrassed and partly touched. Dylan, apparently ready to get going, turned the conversation to business.

"Are you taken care of? Did they tell you to evacuate?" he asked, pulling out his phone. She eyed his phone, but nodded.

"I'm fine. Myrtle is coming by to pick me up. I'll stay with her until this is cleaned up."

Dylan slipped his phone back into his pocket and wrapped his arm around me once more. "If you'll excuse us, Leigha needs to get ready for her sister's wedding, and we're stopping at the police station first so she can press charges."

"Go," she said, stepping back to clear our way with regal forbearance. "I'll expect a dinner invitation by the end of the week."

"You'll have it," Dylan said over shoulder, steering me back to the car.

"You'll regret that later," I said, thinking of Mrs. Carmody and her yappy little dog in Dylan's elegant penthouse.

"No, I won't," he said, his voice tight. Glancing up at him, I realized that despite his easy manner with my neighbor, and his gentleness with me, he was pissed off.

I gave Mrs. Carmody a wave over my shoulder, making an effort to avoid the view of my burning house. From the corner of my eye, I saw that the firefighters seemed to be getting it under control. I hoped it didn't set any of the other houses on fire.

My own stuff had to be a loss; what hadn't burned would be too smoke damaged to salvage. No matter how fast they put out the rest of the fire, it wouldn't save anything.

Suddenly exhausted, I sat back in the plush leather seat, wishing I had time to lay down and take a nap. Dylan slid into the driver's seat and took my hand before he started the car, and we left my latest disaster behind.

CHAPTER THIRTY-SEVEN

DYLAN

L eigha looked so fragile, her eyes closed, lashes dark against her pale cheeks. This was my fault. I'd meant what I'd said to Axel. He'd made the decision not to have Steven arrested on his own, true. But if he'd called me, I would have told him to do exactly the same thing.

Vermin like Steven always had enough for bail. A few hours in prison wasn't enough of a price to pay for hurting Leigha.

I hated the idea that my vengeance had left him free to take even more from her than he already had. If I'd had him arrested he might have done the same thing as soon as he was out on bail. Or maybe a few hours in jail would have convinced him to stay off the radar. I'd never know.

How the fuck had he managed to get away from Tsepov? I knew one thing - unless Tsepov had let him go, Steven would be in deep shit when the Russian tracked him down again.

My business stayed on the clean and legal side, but I

knew what went on in my city, and Axel kept me filled in. His work took him to the dark sides of Vegas more often than he liked.

So I knew that Tsepov was not a man to cross. Ever. If Steven hadn't already gotten out of town, he'd be royally fucked. I couldn't think of anyone who deserved it more.

The next few hours passed in a blur. Leigha looked like she was held together by a thin thread. She gave her statement to the police clearly and with more detail than she'd told me.

I didn't lose it when she described his cutting her with the knife or touching her breast, but I wanted to. Instead, I sat beside Leigha, her hand in mine, feeling the fine tremble as she spoke in a steady, quiet voice. I'd made this hard enough for her, I wasn't going to make it worse.

I brought her home in time for a late lunch in my penthouse. Hard to believe it was only mid-afternoon. She ate a tuna melt with absent attention.

I took in the faint purple bruises under her eyes, the slump of her shoulders, and bumped back the hair and make-up appointment a half an hour. She needed rest more than she needed an elaborate hair style.

Leigha resisted only a little when I carried her to the bedroom and stripped off her shirt and jeans. I tucked her into the bed and climbed in behind her, wrapping my arm around her waist.

"Just close your eyes for a little while," I said. "You'll feel better."

"I can't sleep, Dylan. There's too much in my head."

"Just try. You had a long night and today has been rough. Even if you can't sleep, resting your eyes will help."

She did as I said, and a minute later, she was out. When

I was sure she was asleep, I eased out of the bed and went straight for my phone. Axel answered on the first ring.

"No sign of him," he said. "We're looking, the police are looking. You can bet Tsepov's men are looking."

"We'll need extra security. I don't like the way this guy is fixated on her. Coming back to burn her house wasn't a smart move."

"Can you keep her contained until we've got him?"

"I can keep her in the Delecta," I said. "At least until Monday. But I can't keep her in the penthouse."

"Loosing your touch?"

"Her sister is getting married at six tonight," I said. "She's not going to agree to miss the wedding. Can you cover us?"

"I've got it. I have two guys covering your floor, and I'll coordinate with Russell to get more on the wedding and reception. How's she doing?"

"She's asleep. She got through talking to the police, but she's in shock."

"I can't make it up to her, but I can at least keep her safe until we get Steven."

"This isn't your fault, Axel."

"Not entirely. But I played a part, Dyl."

"So did I," I said. "Now let's just keep that asshole away from her."

I hung up, frustrated that there was nothing I could do to end this situation. I ran a casino and part of Kane enterprises. I had a lot of skills, but hunting down fugitives wasn't one of them. Out there, I'd get in Axel's way more than I'd help. His guys were trained. They'd find Steven.

With nothing else to do until it was time to wake Leigha in an hour, I got back on the phone and called the Audi dealer. A few minutes later they'd agreed to deliver a white Audi TTS convertible roadster with all the extras.

I thought about getting her the R8 Spyder; it had an aggressively sleek look I liked for her, but I had a feeling she'd balk at my giving her a one hundred and thirty thousand dollar car.

I was pushing my luck with the TTS. The dealer assured me that she could exchange it if she didn't like the color, but I thought she'd keep the white. It was elegant, but still sporty. The perfect look for my Leigha.

That item ticked off my list, I sat at my desk and did what I always did when I had a spare second. I opened my laptop and worked.

CHAPTER THIRTY-EIGHT

LEIGHA

D ylan didn't wake me up until the hair stylist arrived. I opened my eyes surprised I'd managed to fall asleep at all. I wasn't much of a napper under normal circumstances, but with all that had happened, my mind and body must have needed an escape.

I sat in a chair in the living room, bundled in a robe, and let the stylist fuss with my hair. I told her I wanted an up-do and zoned out.

Anything she did would look good with my formal dress, and I didn't really care anymore. I just wanted to get the wedding over with and then face the fact that all my worldly possessions could currently fit in my purse.

Across the room, Dylan sat at the desk in the corner of the living room, working on his laptop and occasionally fielding calls. If he wasn't staring into his computer screen, he was pacing in front of the windows, his phone to his ear, speaking in tones low enough that the stylist and I couldn't hear any details.

Once again I was aware of how much work he must be

pushing aside for me. If we stayed together, he couldn't keep doing that. He had too many responsibilities between the Delecta and Kane Enterprises. I knew he must work long hours. Could I handle that?

It was a stupid question - I'd deal with the long hours if they came with Dylan. There were times of the year when I worked crazy hours as well. I was an accountant - January through the end of April were pretty nuts for me. If I could deal with Dylan's work, he'd learn to deal with mine.

As he paced and murmured into his phone, I noticed the stylist devouring the sight of his ass in his worn, well fitting jeans. I almost cleared my throat to get her attention, then changed my mind. He did have a fantastic ass, and who was I to deprive the woman of the opportunity to appreciate it?

I was the one who got to put my hands all over it. If I wanted a relationship with Dylan, I was going to have to get used to all sorts of women ogling his body.

Despite my shock at seeing my house on fire, I was pretty sure I'd even spotted Mrs. Carmody checking him out. I squirmed in my seat at the thought of all the things I could do to Dylan's ass. Biting. Squeezing.

Would he let me spank him? I doubted it. But it was worth asking. Abruptly, I put a halt on that train of thought. I didn't want to get turned on while the stylist had a curling iron in my hair, and I couldn't do anything about it.

My mind drifted as she curled and pinned my hair, then was replaced by the make-up artist who got busy working on covering my bruises. I saw a pair of long white gloves laying over the back of the couch and thought of Lola.

I should get a good insurance settlement for the house. I'd called my agent on the way to the police station, and he assured me that it wouldn't take long to work out the details.

I'd have to replace all my clothes, but I'd covered the contents of my house generously.

Most of the time, I tried to save money, but I'd sprung for the best homeowner's policy I could get. It had been my first house, and I'd wanted to protect it.

Which meant I should have plenty of money to pay for a new wardrobe. I wondered if I'd be able to afford Lola. Not if she only did personal shopping for the kinds of clothes Dylan had bought me. But if she worked with all of Neiman Marcus's inventory, I could make that fit my budget as long as I went with classic pieces that wouldn't go out of style a few months after I bought them.

Lola had been a genius for finding things that looked good on my curvy body. Imagining my new wardrobe, I barely noticed the time passing. Before I knew it, the make-up artist was done, and it was time to get dressed.

Dylan showed her out as I headed straight for the bathroom mirror. My hair was amazing, pulled smoothly back from my face and up into a high knot of curls and twists. It was both dramatic and fanciful; a perfect match for my strapless black dress and its silver embroidered flowers.

The make-up artist must have been a genius. Or she'd been packing industrial strength spackle. I saw no sign of the bruises on my face, only smooth, pore-less skin. She'd done something to bring out my cheekbones and shaded my eyes in a deep purple-blue that would set off the dress and made my gray eyes seem to glow.

If I had the time and budget, I'd have those two show up every day before I left the house. I knew I'd never have the patience to do it, even if I could afford it, but it was a fun idea. Shrugging out of my robe, I was wrestling with the black satin bustier that went under my gown when Dylan entered the bedroom.

Quickly, before he could see my awkward struggle to fasten the hooks, I got the last three done and wrenched the thing into place. When he saw me, standing in front of the bathroom sink wearing the satin bustier, matching panties, and the sparkly silver heels, he stopped dead.

"Please tell me that's what you're wearing tonight, and we're staying home."

I grinned. "Sorry. I wish we could. But if you behave and let me get dressed, I'll let you take it off later."

"You'll let me take it off even if I don't behave." His devilish grin was enough to send a bolt of heat straight between my legs. Of course I would. Any smart woman would do whatever Dylan asked if he smiled at her like that. I already knew how amazing he was in bed. And I was a smart women.

Proving that he was an intelligent man, he leaned in to me and kissed my cheek, whispering, "I want to pin you to the wall and fuck you until you're screaming my name. But that can wait until after the wedding."

Stepping back, he said, "I have something for you. I was going to wait until you were ready, but now I think I want to see you wearing it while you're dressed exactly like that."

He picked up a flat, black velvet box and opened it to reveal a sparking diamond necklace with matching earrings and bracelet. I gasped, taking a step back in surprise.

The necklace was fashioned of diamonds arranged in the shape of flowers, intricately mounted so that the piece appeared to be made entirely of sparkling stones with no metal holding it together. Only a little longer than a collar, it would hug my throat in a very expensive embrace.

"Dylan, seriously, this is too much," I said, looking at the open jewelry box with a combination of helpless avarice and exasperation. "You can't buy me diamonds. You can't. It's crazy."

"How do you know these are diamonds? Maybe this is a really good fake," he asked, moving behind me to fasten the necklace around my neck. I didn't need to look in the mirror to know that it was a perfect complement to the dress.

"Is it?" I asked, relieved at the suggestion. He laughed and decorated one earlobe with one of the matching earrings.

"Of course not," he said, humor shaking in his voice. "Do you think I'd buy you fakes? It's from the Sunflower collection by Harry Winston. Lola says they've been sold out since the collection debuted two years ago, but she had a line on this set. It's perfect with the dress."

"But you can't just..." I trailed off, not sure what to say. It seemed obvious to me. We'd only known each other a few days. His buying me extravagant gifts was over the top. Except that he clearly seemed to think it was fine. Proving me right, he said,

"I can, Leigha. I know this is hard for you to understand. You've worked for everything you have, and you know the value of money. I like that about you. I like that you're not trying to get everything you can out of me. The problem is that just makes me want to spoil you more."

He took my wrist in his hand and lifted it in front of him so he could lay the sparkling line of diamond sunflowers against my skin. The bracelet was a sculpture of glittering stones. I had a feeling the jewelry he'd bought so casually was worth more than my house had been before Steven had burned it to the ground.

"Dylan," I said, unable to stop myself from laughing. Taking advantage of my inability to protest further, he went on,

"I don't know how to say this without sounding like an arrogant douche, but you do know I have a lot of money, right?"

"I know you're a billionaire, but -"

"Leigha, you're an accountant, you know what being a billionaire means. Stuff like this has no impact on my life, other than the pleasure of giving it to you."

"But -"

"Stop." He kissed my temple. "We need to go. If I stay near you one more second, I'm going to forget all my good intentions and make sure we miss the wedding. Finish getting dressed and meet me by the elevator."

He was gone before I could think of something else to say. I realized after he left that he'd still been in his jeans and button down. He must have been planning to change in the other bedroom.

Catching sight of myself in the mirror, I froze. In my satin lingerie, my breasts overflowing the bodice, my waist cinched in, my neck, wrist, and ears dripping in diamond flowers, I looked like a debauched princess. The thought of what Dylan might do when he had me alone later sent a shiver down my spine.

He was right, we had to leave before we changed our minds and decided to skip the wedding. I'm not sure I could have cared less about Christie's ceremony or reception, especially considering the pig she was marrying. But my Mom had to leave the next day to go home, and I didn't want to let her down by blowing off the wedding.

Mindful of the spike heels of my sandals, I stepped into the dress and pulled it up my body. With a little shifting and wiggling, I managed to get the zipper up. Grabbing my tiny clutch, I left the room to meet Dylan.

My breath caught as I closed the door of the penthouse

and caught sight of him standing in front of the elevator. He wore his tux with an innate elegance that did nothing to hide the strength of the body beneath. Yum.

His green eyes flashed when he saw me, the look on his face carnal enough to make my knees weak. We would definitely be leaving the reception early.

The doors slid soundlessly open the second he pressed the button. I joined him inside, standing beside him, my fingers twining with his as if we'd been holding hands for decades instead of mere days.

As the elevator began its smooth decent, I had the feeling that I wasn't just heading out for the evening, I was about to begin an entirely new life.

CHAPTER THIRTY-NINE

LEIGHA

Spying the gorgeous bracelet on my wrist, I decided to try one more time to talk to Dylan about his extravagance. I was finally ready to admit this was more than a weekend fling. I cared about him, and I didn't want money to come between us.

"I know that you like buying me things, and I think I must be crazy to be saying this, but you have to stop."

Dylan didn't say anything, just looked down at me and raised one eyebrow. I went on, trying to explain in fumbling words.

"It's just that you don't need to do this. And it feels unbalanced. Now that my house is gone, I need to get my life organized and I don't want to feel like I'm a bottomless pit of need in your life. I want to be on equal footing. Do you understand?"

He stared at me, his gaze penetrating, giving me the unsettling feeling that he was reading my mind. After what felt like an eternity, he said, "I'll take a break from buying you things. For a while, not forever. And only if you promise me two things."

"What two things?" I asked, suspicious of his easy capitulation.

"One, you accept the car that's downstairs in the garage."

"What kind of car?" I asked. If the man could go overboard with a dress, what would he do when he decided to buy a car? His Maserati wasn't exactly a Ford Focus.

"An Audi TTS roadster, white with camel leather interior."

Wow. I wanted to say no. At least, the good girl in me wanted to say no. The rest of me was too busy drooling.

"Is that the convertible?" I asked, afraid I sounded too greedy.

"Yes."

Oh, I was in trouble. I liked that car. A lot. I'd looked at the TT a few years before, but it had been both impractical and way out of my budget. Every time I saw one, I drooled a little. How had he known? I shouldn't accept it. But I was going to.

"What's the second condition?" I asked, stalling.

"Agree to the car first," he answered. The elevator hit the ground floor with a barely perceptible shudder. Dylan reached out and hit the STOP button. Suddenly nervous, I said,

"Okay. I shouldn't, but okay." Then, after an awkward pause, "Thank you." He rewarded me with a brilliant smile.

"You're welcome, sweetheart."

"And the second condition?" I asked, a little anxious.

"Move in with me."

"What?" What? I couldn't move in with him. "I can't

move in with you," I said, my voice loud and high pitched in the small space.

"Why not? You don't have anywhere to go right now. And it's going to take time to get the insurance settled. So stay with me."

"Are you asking me to move in, or just to stay for a while?" I asked, suspicious.

"Whichever one will get you to say yes."

"You're freaking me out," I confessed.

"No I'm not. You *think* you should be freaked out. You think this is too much. But if you take a deep breath, I bet you'll realize you're *not* actually freaked out. A part of you knows this is right. That we're right together."

His eyes on mine were intense, yet calm, as if he could will his own certainty into me. Closing my eyes to shut him out, I did what he'd suggested and took a deep breath, or as deep as I could in the tight bustier.

With nothing to see but the dark of my closed eyes, I tried to steady myself. Was I nervous about this because I was scared? Because I'd never imagined a man like Dylan would ever be interested in me? Or because this was all sex and the thrill of adventure, destined to wear off as soon as we went back to our normal lives?

I thought of the past three days together. It had started with need and want. I'd needed a date. And the moment we'd met, we'd both wanted sex. That was the simple part. If this was just about sex, I would have been shouting yes.

But I knew myself. I couldn't live with a man if all we had was sex. Even the best orgasm wouldn't make up for all the annoyances that came with sharing living space with a virtual stranger.

And if sex was all he wanted, he could install me in one of his hotel rooms and have me close, but not in his space.

So this was more than sex. I took another deep breath, remembering my favorite times with Dylan that weekend. Not counting the sex - I'd already covered that part.

It wasn't the shopping, though that had been fun. And it wasn't walking into the rehearsal dinner and seeing jealousy on the other women's faces. No, it was the conversation over lunch the day before. His hand rubbing my back in the hospital. The way he'd brought me to my house that morning, knowing I'd need to see the fire for myself, then brought me back home and tucked me into bed, already knowing I'd needed a nap.

It was his intelligence, his kindness, his sweetness. It was that beneath the movie star good looks, he was a man worth loving. And if he saw even a fraction of that in me, I really would be crazy to walk away just because I was scared. Still, I was nothing if not sensible, even when I was ready to take a huge risk. Opening my eyes, I said,

"Okay. I'll move in with you. But once my insurance stuff is worked out, we'll talk about how it's going and if either of us is having second thoughts, we'll make other arrangements."

"Deal."

Dylan's arms came around me, drawing me close, the look in his eyes one of heated tenderness. At that moment, I was ready to ditch the wedding and head right back upstairs. His lips took mine in a kiss of pure possession. I kissed him back, ready to be brave, to claim this man as my own.

I was trying to wipe the edge of my lips discreetly when the Dylan pressed the button to release the elevator doors. They slid open to reveal my mother, whose eyes widened for a moment before she let loose with a wide smile.

"I was wondering where you two were. Come on, we're

almost late. Though you know Christie won't be ready on time. But we should be there. You look beautiful, Leigha, just wonderful."

She kept up a steady stream of chatter as she led us to the Delecta's wedding chapel. Taking in the elegant room, it was clear the casino did a big business in weddings. We slid into our aisle after Dylan scowled away the usher who tried to take my arm. Not too many minutes later, the music kicked in and the ceremony began.

Thankfully, it was a quick wedding. Neither the bride nor groom was particularly religious or spiritual, and they stuck with the basics. A few words, some back and forth on the vows, a kiss and they were done. I was ready to get to the reception, then escape to be alone with Dylan as soon as possible.

I was thinking about luring him into another dark hall-way, though this time we'd keep it clean, when my mother linked her arm with mine and drew me away from Dylan. He caught my free hand in his and said, "Don't leave my sight, not until Steven is in custody."

"I won't," I said, letting my mother pull me toward the chapel exit.

"Dylan can do without you for a minute or two," she said, tucking my arm in hers as we walked. "I've never seen you look so beautiful, honey. You're glowing. Is it love? Or just really amazing sex?"

"Mom!" I was a fully grown woman, but my Mom could still make me blush.

"I think it's both," she said with a satisfied smile. I remained silent, admitting nothing as she went on, "I knew you'd hook him, honey."

"Mom, he's not a fish," I said, my need to defend Dylan forcing me out of my mortified silence.

"No, he's a whale." She giggled. "Seriously, honey, I knew you'd get him. The way he looks at you. Whew!" She pretended to fan herself.

"I'm moving in with him," I admitted. She patted my arm.

"Good girl."

"It's not about that," I protested, worried that she thought I was after Dylan for his money.

"What?" she asked, "The money or the sex? I know you, Leigha, so I know it's not about the money. Anyway, greedy bitches don't get men like that. The only way to get a man like Dylan is just to be you."

It was exactly what I needed to hear. Most of my uncertainty over my relationship with Dylan melted into a warm glow in my chest. I was lifting an arm to hug my Mom when I heard a shout off to the left. Curious, I turned to see Steven bearing down on us, wildly waving a gun in one hand.

I backed away in horror, shouting Dylan's name and trying to shove my mother behind me. I was taller and bigger, but she had a mother's need to protect her child, and we ended up scuffling when we should have been running. All the while, Steven came closer, shouting in unintelligible bursts.

I couldn't see Dylan in the suddenly screaming, milling crowd on the casino floor. From the sides of the vast room men in identical black suits melted out of the sea of people, some of them speaking into clear plastic earpieces, a few brandishing guns. They would have been comforting if they hadn't been so far away.

In slow motion I watched Steven raise the gun and aim it at me, shouting, "I'm going to kill you, you bitch."

Out of nowhere, Dylan launched himself through the

air, catching Steven in his gut, taking him to the floor in a tangle of limbs. A blast echoed as the gun went off, followed by a crash as the bullet hit a chandelier above.

The impact of hitting the floor jarred the gun from Steven's hand where it was picked up by one of the black suited security guards. Shards of crystal fell around us as I rushed toward them, heedless of the danger in my need to get to Dylan. A hard arm caught me in the midsection, dragging me back. I struggled until I heard a familiar voice in my ear.

"Stay back Leigha. Dylan's fine," Axel said.

"How did Steven get in here?" I demanded.

"We're working on figuring that out. The police are already here. He'll be gone in a minute."

I didn't want to wait. I wanted to talk to him before he was taken away. Wrenching back from Axel, I headed for Dylan and Steven. Axel was clearly unwilling to wrestle me down because he followed without further discussion.

Dylan held Steven on the floor with a knee to his neck. Steven wasn't struggling, but Dylan scowled at me and said,

"Leigha, get back." Looking at Axel, he growled, "What the fuck?"

"I want to talk to him," I said.

"No," Dylan answered. "There's nothing this asshole has to say that you need to hear."

"Dylan, I want to talk to him. Please." Dylan scowled at me, but slid his knee back and pulled Steven to a sitting position. Axel moved behind Steven, producing a set of handcuffs. He secured Steven's hands with the smooth skill born of practice.

"Why?" I asked Steven, finally meeting his enraged brown eyes. "You stole from me. You burned my house to the ground. Now you try to kill me." Behind me, I heard my mother gasp. "Why?" I demanded. "Why me? What did I do to you?"

"This is all your fault, you stupid, fucking bitch. Everything was fine until your fucking ten grand. That was the money that put me in the hole with Tsepov. I haven't won a hand of cards since I bet that money. You killed my luck and then you couldn't make it right. Burning down your house should have broken the curse, but it didn't. I need you dead."

I stared at him, dumbfounded. "You did all this because you think I'm responsible for your bad luck at cards?"

"It's you. It's your fault. All of it." He started to mumble under his breath. Now that I was closer, I could smell the sour scent of stale liquor coming off him. I looked over at Dylan, who had come to his feet and moved beside me.

"He's insane," I said, hearing the amazement in my voice. "Completely nuts. He tried to kill me because he had bad luck at cards after betting the money he stole from me? Is that what he just said? Seriously?"

"It is," Dylan agreed sliding his arms around me from behind. Abruptly the jolt of adrenaline from seeing the gun faded, and I leaned back into Dylan's warmth. Together, we watched five policemen separate the crowd as they headed for Steven. His prone body disappeared under the swarm of blue. They yanked him to his feet, escorted him across the main floor of the Delecta, and out of my life.

I was sure I'd have to deal with him again when he went to trial, but for now I was free from the threat of further destruction.

"Don't do that again," I said to Dylan, turning to brush a stray piece of carpet fluff off his sleeve. "He could have shot you."

"He was *going* to shoot you," Dylan said. "Don't try to

stop me from protecting you again, Leigha. I won't do it. You're mine. I'd take a bullet if I had to."

My heart swelled. Dylan was sweet and terrifying at the same time.

"Okay, how about I just stay away from crazy men with guns, and then you won't have to go near any bullets?"

"That works for me," he said, pressing a kiss to my lips. I wanted more, but we were surrounded by people, one of whom was my mother. As I leaned into his arms I heard my sister's shrill voice say,

"Is the drama over yet? I'd like to get back to my wedding!"

Typical. I almost get shot and she's worried about it interrupting her party. Any other day she might have bothered me, but not today. Not when I'd just decided to move in with an amazing man who'd saved my life.

"Come on," Dylan said, wrapping his arm around my shoulders in a possessive hold. "Let's go. I want to dance with you at the wedding."

That I could do. Though the way he said 'wedding' made me a little nervous. Three days and I'd agreed to move in. He wasn't going to get any ideas about weddings, was he?

Mentally, I shrugged. I was done worrying about the future, at least for now. Life was too good to stress. Instead, I was going to hang on tight to Dylan and enjoy the ride.

EPILOGUE
LEIGHA

Four Months Later

I sat at the bar studying my mostly full appletini and waiting for Dylan. I hadn't been back to this place since the night I'd met Dylan here. Tonight, another Thursday, it wasn't crowded. I was even wearing another navy blue dress, though Lola had picked this one out, and it looked much better on me than the dress I'd been wearing the night Dylan had swept into my life.

It was funny to be here, sitting on the same stool, remembering how miserable I'd been until Dylan sat beside me and asked about my day. Since we'd met I'd known happiness I hadn't believed possible, even in those first few days with Steven's video and my house burning down.

I never ended up moving out of Dylan's penthouse. By the time the insurance was settled, and I had a big fat check to spend on a new home, I'd been at Dylan's for a month and couldn't imagine wanting to leave.

I'd worried that he might be ready to have his space

back. After all, when we'd met Dylan had a reputation as a player. A part of me had wondered if he really could have changed so thoroughly in such a short time. That small, doubting voice in my head couldn't quite believe I'd gotten so lucky.

Dylan had solved that problem in his typical no bullshit way. Coming home the night after I'd met with the insurance adjuster, he'd looked at the envelope with the check sitting on the counter and immediately knew what it was. Not wasting time, he'd cornered me in the living room.

"Is that the check for your house?" he'd asked, his green eyes examining my face. I'd nodded. He came closer, backing me into his desk, caging me with his arms. "And?"

"And," I said, swallowing to work up my nerve, "I can move out now. If you want me to." My stomach twisted in a queasy knot. I needed to give him an out, needed to know I'd made it easy for him.

"Is that what you want?" he asked.

Unable to speak, I just shook my head.

"Then what do you want?" he'd asked gently, tracing one finger over my cheekbone. Searching for courage, I looked him in the eyes and said,

"I want you. I want to stay."

He'd closed his arms around me, pulling me tight to his body and whispered in my ear.

"Good. Because I don't think I could let you leave. I love you Leigha Carmichael."

Melting into him, I'd whispered back, "I love you too, Dylan Kane."

That had been the real beginning. That moment was when we stopped hiding our hearts and admitted how much we wanted to be together.

Since then, life had fallen into an easy rhythm. We both

worked full days, Dylan often busy in his office late into the night. I usually waited up for him, sometimes falling asleep on the couch in front of the TV. I'd wake to feel him lifting me in his arms, carrying me to our bed.

Sometimes Dylan had social events we needed to go to, part work and part play. I enjoyed these far more than I'd expected, mostly because I was on Dylan's arm and sporting whatever divine outfit Lola had put together for me.

She was my new savior where clothes were concerned. I'd never loved shopping in the past, always too self conscious about my shape to have any fun trying things on. But Lola knew what would flatter me, and she had a wonderful eye for color. I asked her for help replacing all my clothes and she'd outfitted me with a wardrobe to kill for, even before I knew I wouldn't need all the insurance money for a new house.

I had to admit since I'd officially moved in with Dylan I'd gone a little nuts over shoes. True to my accountant's heart, I'd socked most of it away in reliable investments. But my new closet was huge, and I'd discovered I loved expensive heels. Mostly for me, but I couldn't help but love the look Dylan got when he saw me in a sweet pair of sexy heels. Really, that look was for me too.

My phone beeped in front of me and I checked the screen.

On my way. Got held up on a call.

Dylan. I'd learned that, as I'd suspected, that first weekend aside, he worked a lot. But I rarely had to ask him to make time for me. He always remembered our plans and kept me posted if he was late or had to reschedule.

I did my best to be understanding, aware that when tax season rolled around, he'd be the one getting texts and rushed phone calls about me working until midnight.

We'd had our only real fight the first time he left Vegas for a business trip. He'd wanted me to join him. I said no. If I hadn't had my job, I would have loved to fly East to meet his brother and cousin. But I had clients and responsibilities. I couldn't just skip town in the middle of the week.

Dylan had given in eventually. I think it helped that things were better at work. I suspected either Dylan had gone behind my back and spoken to my slimy boss, or my boss had found out who I was living with.

Either way, he'd been keeping his distance and treating me with cautious respect. He also sucked at his job and the higher-ups had noticed. I suspected he'd be replaced any day now.

I felt Dylan at my back before I saw him. His arms came around me from behind, pulling me back into his chest as his head dropped beside mine. He kissed the shell of my ear and whispered,

"Sorry I'm late."

"It's okay," I said, turning my head so I could press my lips to his. "I haven't been here long. Just sitting here thinking."

"Hmm? Remembering the night we met? How I lured you up to my office and took shameless advantage of you?"

He winked at me, giving me an exaggerated lear so unlike his normal, seductive smile that I burst out laughing.

"If your game had been that bad," I said, "You never would have gotten me off this stool."

"It's a good thing I knew exactly what to say to get you alone."

That was the understatement of the century. What if I had said no to him then? I would have missed so much. Watching him as he took the stool beside me, wearing a well cut gray suit, his dark hair sexily mussed from the long day, I knew there was no way I would have told him no.

I'd had my stupid moments. The whole debacle with Steven case in point. But even at my worst, I never would have been foolish enough to turn Dylan down. And that was without knowing what a good man he was. How sweet. How unbelievably hot in bed. And how loyal. How loving.

I waited for Dylan to order a drink, but he gave a dismissive signal to the bartender standing at alert a few feet away. The bartender left to polish glass on the far side of the room and I looked at Dylan in confusion. We didn't usually hang out in bars unless it was part of an event for Dylan's work. So I was a little curious as to why Dylan had asked me to meet him here, in the bar where we'd met, and yet still hadn't ordered a drink.

Clearing his throat, he said, "You're probably wondering why I asked you to meet me here instead of my office."

He sounded nervous, completely unlike himself. I realized with a jolt that I'd never seen Dylan nervous. I straightened on my stool, my appletini forgotten, alert to what might be going on. I had no clue. Trying to hide my confusion, I said,

"The thought crossed my mind."

He reached out and took my hand in his, his green eyes locking on mine. "I saw you that night sitting here, and I knew you were someone special. I only talked to you for a few minutes before I had to have you in my bed. What I didn't know was how quickly I'd fall in love with you. And how certain I'd be that you're the only woman I'll ever want."

Releasing my hand, he drew something from his pocket. My heart stuttered in my chest, and my brain froze. My eyes must have widened comically when I saw the black velvet box in his hand because he smiled and said,

"Will you?"

"Ask me the right way," I said through a tight throat, too nervous to assume he was asking what I hoped he was asking.

Standing, he tugged me off the stool, then dropped to one knee before me. Taking my left hand in his, he said,

"Leigh Carmichael, you're the only woman I've ever loved. I want to make a life with you, have children with you, and grow old with you. You're the best thing that ever happened to me. Will you be my wife?"

I managed to squeak out a 'Yes' as tears welled in my eyes. Dylan slid the ring on my finger as he stood, pulling me into his arms. I lifted my head, meeting his lips with mine. His kiss was fierce, possessive, and filled with love. On the other side of the bar, I heard the pop of a champagne bottle opening. Two glasses clinked beside us.

Dylan let me go just long enough to pick up my champagne and hand it to me. I discretely wiped lipgloss from my lower lip, but ignored the champagne in favor of checking out my ring.

It was huge. I didn't know enough about jewelry to guess at the carat weight, but I knew big from small. This was bigger than big, just on the classy side of too much.

Set in platinum, I was sure Dylan would have chosen the more expensive platinum over white gold, the ring had a large, round, brilliantly clear center diamond surrounded by a geometric bezel frame decorated with small diamonds, set in a pave band with yet more small diamonds. It was almost blinding as it sparkled on my hand.

I had a habit of complaining to Dylan when he spent too much money on me. Four months hadn't been enough to break lifelong habits of sensible economy. But I wasn't going to say a word about what this ring must have cost. I knew Dylan too well to think he'd get anything less than the absolute best for my engagement ring.

Raising my eyes to his, I said, "It's beautiful. I love it. And I love you."

"Maybe this wasn't the most romantic place to propose," he said, again sounding a little uncertain. Was it possible even the mighty Dylan Kane got a little off balance where marriage was concerned? To stop him from worrying I raised a finger and pressed it to his lips.

"No," I said. "This is the perfect place. Who would have thought when I was crying into my drink that I'd end up here, in love with the most wonderful man in the world, ready to spend the rest of my life with him."

That must have been the right thing to say because Dylan's uncertainty vanished. He scooped me up into his arms and turned for the exit, saying over his shoulder,

"Have the champagne sent up to the penthouse, but tell them to leave it in the hall."

"Are we skipping our dinner reservations?" I asked, my lips moving against the warm skin of Dylan's neck.

"We don't have any. That was a lie to get you to the bar. We're having dinner delivered. Later. Much later. For now, I have a covered plate of appetizers and a very empty bed."

I shivered in his arms. It was just like that first night when he'd lured me from the bar with the promise of food and fed me savory treats, seducing me with his eyes and his words. Except that time, we'd had to rush out after only a kiss. Not tonight. Tonight we had all the time in the world to be together. We had the rest of our lives.

CHAPTER ONE
CHLOE

I lay on the couch reading a book on my tablet; the screen dimmed so the light wouldn't give me away. Beside me, a mug of tea steamed, scenting the air with herbs and flowers. I was trying to relax. Tea, a good book, sacking out on the couch. I should have been totally chilled.

Instead, every muscle in my body was tense. The house was brand new, but each creak sent shivers down my spine. I wasn't supposed to be here. No one was.

I'd left the lights off, sneaking around in the shadows to set up my sleeping bag on the couch and brewing my tea using the built-in hot water spout in the kitchen. Dinner had been a drive-through burger and fries, the now empty bag sitting on the floor beside me.

The idea had been to hide out, try to calm down somewhere safe, and then figure out what to do. So far, it wasn't working. I'd taken care of the hiding out somewhere safe part. At least I hoped I had. No one who might be looking for me would be looking here.

As far as figuring out what to do? I had no clue. It wasn't even my mess I was running from. It was my baby brother's. I'd been taking care of him our whole lives.

It had been suggested to me, more than once, that maybe it was time to stop. But he was my brother. My only real family. I wouldn't turn my back on him.

The glare of headlights flashed across the front windows of the two story house, sending terror crashing through me. No one should be here. There weren't any residents in this neighborhood. It was a new construction community, and I was squatting in the model home.

A truck pulled into the driveway and idled. Struggling to catch my breath, I slid off the couch and moved to hide behind its bulk. Should I try to sneak out the back door?

I'd parked a few streets away so my car in the drive wouldn't be obvious, and I'd have to pick my way across the construction site in the dark. But that was preferable to facing the people looking for me.

Suddenly my bright idea about hiding in the model home didn't seem like such a good plan. I was completely isolated, surrounded by acres of mud and silent construction vehicles. No one to hear me scream. No one to help.

The silence of the truck shutting off, followed by the heavy thunk of a door closing had my heart thundering in my chest. What to do?

I crab walked backwards into the kitchen and slid across the hardwood floor to hide behind the island. The houses here all had open floor plans. Attractive and practical unless you were trying to hide.

I lost the chance to make a run for the bedrooms when the front door swung open and the lights flipped on.

Whoever was here had a key, then. That improved my chances a lot. At the realization of who it must be, my heart calmed, then sank.

Taking a risk, I peaked out around the side of the kitchen island to see who was at the front door. In the glare of the lights I saw a tall figure with broad shoulders, long legs, a lean waist, and a familiar shock of messy blond hair. Sam. Before I could stand up to reveal myself, he spoke.

"I already called the police, so I suggest you get your ass out here and explain yourself before you get arrested."

I jumped to my feet, wishing with all my heart that I wasn't wearing my now very wrinkled suit. It was bad enough that Sam was way out of my league. He didn't need to see me looking like I'd been sleeping in my work clothes.

"Sam, it's me. Don't call the police."

"Chloe?" he said in surprise. Belatedly I noticed he held a gun at his side, his arm tense and ready. He lifted the gun and did something to it before he shoved it in his waistband behind his back. "What the hell, Chloe? I could have shot you."

"I didn't know you had a gun," I said. Not really the point. And kind of a dumb thing to say, but my head was spinning. For a moment, while he was holding that gun, he hadn't looked like my Sam at all. He'd been menacing. Scary.

"Yeah, I have a gun," he said. "And I didn't call the cops. I called Axel. Hold on a sec. And don't move," he barked when I turned to go back to the couch.

He was angry. I couldn't remember the last time I'd seen Sam angry. At least not at me. Sam never got mad at me. Not wanting to piss him off further, I stayed where I was, between the kitchen and the living room, and watched him make a call.

"It's me," he said, scowling in my direction. "Don't worry about it. It was Chloe." A pause. "I have no idea, but I'm going to find out. Yeah, later."

Shoving the phone in his pocket, he pointed to the couch and said, "Sit." I did.

"Did you forget that I had an alarm put on the gate and the spec houses after we had those problems with vandalism last month?" he asked.

Damn it. I had forgotten. Normally, as Sam's assistant, I would have set up something like that, but one of Sam's best friends was Axel Sinclair, who ran the western division of Sinclair Security. Sam had taken care of the arrangements himself. And since I was rarely on site without Sam, it had slipped my mind. Deciding to keep my mouth shut for the moment, I said nothing.

"What are you doing here? Why aren't you at your apartment? What happened? Chloe, are you alright?"

At the open concern in his last question, I burst into tears. I could have held out against anger, but I had no defenses against worry. Not from Sam. I clapped my hands to my eyes trying to stem the flow of tears and calm my hitching breaths when I heard him swear and get up. A moment later he was sitting beside me, pulling me into his arms.

My head fell against his chest and I melted, giving up for the moment on trying to be strong. Sam was here. As long as Sam was here, I was safe. At least for right now.

I'd been Sam Logan's assistant for three years and had been head over heels in love with him for almost all of them.

Sam was smart. Handsome in a way that meant he looked equally good dressed for the construction site as he did in a suit. And he couldn't have been less interested in me.

He was a great boss. A good friend. And I knew he cared about me. He had to, otherwise why would he be sitting here letting me cry all over him? But he'd never love me.

I knew that. I'd watched him date a succession of tall, slender, dramatically beautiful women over the years in a series of casually monogamous relationships. And having seen every one of his girlfriends up close at one time or another, I knew why he'd never look at me.

I was a nice person. I was loyal, caring, and fun. But I wasn't tall, skinny, or beautiful. I guessed I was pretty enough. I'd had a few boyfriends who seemed to think so.

My hair and my skin were my best features. My skin was smooth and almost pore less. I'd tell you what moisturizer I use, but it wouldn't help since it's been this way my whole life, no matter what I put on it. And while my hair was a boring light brown, it was shiny, with curl and body.

The rest of me was a bit of a let down. If I was feeling generous, I'd call myself curvy. Very curvy. Most days I just felt plump. And I was kind of short. If you picture the opposite of Sam's tall, slender, model girlfriends, you'd get me.

So we were friends, but that was all we'd ever be. Most days I was okay with that. I really hadn't dated much in the past two years, once I finally admitted to myself how I felt about Sam, because every other man just didn't measure up.

Right then, terrified and tucked safely into Sam's arms, I wasn't regretting that he'd never love me. I was just grateful he was there.

When I'd run from the back patio of my apartment and snuck to where I'd parked my car on the street, I'd considered going to Sam. But I'd thought he'd said he'd be out tonight. And I didn't want to tell him what was going on until I had a chance to think it through myself. Too late for that now.

My tears gradually faded, and I forced myself to pull away from the heat of Sam's arms. He smelled like spice and citrus. Masculine and strong. Sexy. I wiped at my face and told myself to focus.

Yes, Sam is hot. I know that. I see him every day, and every day he's hot. It was not the time to get distracted by how good he looked. And smelled.

Trying to get a little distance, I stood and moved to sit in the arm chair facing the couch. Sam scowled at me again.

"Tell me what's going on Chloe. Now," he said, clearly out of patience.

"Nolan is missing," I admitted. "He didn't come home Saturday night, and he's not answering his phone. I thought maybe he was just-"

"Being typically irresponsible?" Sam said in a dry tone.

Sam wasn't a big fan of my brother. He thought Nolan needed to grow up and stop leaning on me. Sam was probably right. But he didn't understand our relationship. I ignored Sam's comment and went on.

"I got home after work tonight a little later than usual and I had to park a few spots away. I was going in the back because it was closer and I had groceries when I saw people in my apartment. I almost went right in because I thought they might be with Nolan. But then I saw one of them holding a gun."

It had been dizzying, the sway between relief that Nolan was home and shock that there were strangers with weapons in my little apartment.

"I listened to them for a few minutes. They were looking for Nolan. But then they said they wanted to take me in, too."

"Take you in where?" Sam demanded, sitting up straight on the couch.

"I don't know. They had accents, and it was hard to understand what they were saying."

"Did you get a good look at him? At any of them?"

"Not really, I was outside on the patio, trying to stay out of sight behind the blinds. There were three of them. Tall. Dark hair. The one with the gun talked the most."

"What kind of accent?"

"I'm not sure. European. Not French or Spanish. Maybe Russian. Something Eastern European, I think."

"Fuck. Are you sure?"

"No," I said, suddenly annoyed.

I'd done the best I could, but I'd been confused and then scared shitless when they'd said they'd settle for taking me if they couldn't get Nolan. It hadn't occurred to me to stick around and see what else I could find out.

I'd turned and run back to my car as quietly as I could, glad I'd left my purse and briefcase in the back seat.

"Sorry, Chloe. I'm just worried. This doesn't sound like one of Nolan's usual fuck-ups."

"No, it doesn't."

Normally I'd bristle at Sam referring to Nolan's occasional issues as 'fuck-ups'. Nolan had made a few mistakes. In the two years he'd been living with me in Vegas, he'd had a DUI and almost lost his license for reckless driving. Helping him with that one had taken a chunk out of my savings.

He'd also been fired from two jobs before he'd landed one at the tech start-up where he was currently working. Or had been until a few weeks ago. I'd called Monday morning to find out if he was there, only to hear that he'd been let go almost a month before.

My brother was smart. He was also impulsive and restless. I loved him, but even I could admit it was past time for him to grow up. Before that could happen, I had to find him. Sam pulled his phone back out of his pocket and started to dial. Alarmed, I said,

"Stop, who are you calling?"

"Axel," he said, looking at me as if I was a little slow. Of course he'd be calling Axel.

"You can't call Axel."

"Why not?" Sam asked, starting to look exasperated.

ALSO BY IVY LAYNE

Scandals of the Bad Boy Billionaires

The Billionaire's Secret Heart (Novella)

The Billionaire's Secret Love (Novella)

The Billionaire's Pet

The Billionaire's Promise

The Rebel Billionaire

The Billionaire's Secret Kiss (Novella)

The Billionaire's Angel

Other Books By Ivy Layne

The Wedding Rescue

The Courtship Maneuver

The Temptation Trap

Don't Miss Out on New Releases, Exclusive Giveaways, and More!!

Join Ivy's Readers Group!

ivylayne.com/readers-group

ABOUT IVY LAYNE

Ivy Layne has had her nose stuck in a book since she first learned to decipher the English language. Sometime in her early teens, she stumbled across her first Romance, and the die was cast. Though she pretended to pay attention to her creative writing professors, she dreamed of writing steamy romance instead of literary fiction. These days, she's neck deep in alpha heroes and the smart, sexy women who love them.

Married to her very own alpha hero (who rubs her back after a long day of typing, but also leaves his socks on the floor). Ivy lives in the mountains of North Carolina where she and her other half are having a blast raising two energetic little boys. Aside from her family, Ivy's greatest loves are coffee and chocolate, preferably together.

VISIT IVY
Facebook.com/AuthorIvyLayne
Instagram.com/authorivylayne/
www.ivylayne.com
books@ivylayne.com

CPSIA information can be obtained
at www.ICGtesting.com
Printed in the USA
LVHW080043200520
656093LV00018B/2782